LED ASTRAY

AND

THE SPHINX

MORE WILDSIDE CLASSICS

LED ASTRAY

AND

THE SPHINX

OCTAVE FEUILLET

WILDSIDE PRESS

LED ASTRAY and THE SPHINX

This edition published 2005 by Wildside Press, LLC.
www.wildsidepress.com

CONTENTS

LED ASTRAY

CHAPTER I.

A Graphic Description.

George L— to Paul B., Paris
Rozel, *15th September.*

It's nine o'clock in the evening, my dear friend, and you have just arrived from Germany. They hand you my letter, the postmark of which informs you at once that I am absent from Paris. You indulge in a gesture of annoyance, and call me a vagabond. Nevertheless, you settle down in your best armchair, you open my letter, and you hear that I have been for the past five days domesticated in a flour mill in Lower Normandy. In a flour mill! What the duse can he be doing in a mill? A wrinkle appears on your forehead, your eyebrows are drawn together; you lay down my letter for a moment; you attempt to penetrate this mystery by the unaided power of your imagination. Suddenly a playful expression beams upon your countenance; your mouth expresses the irony of a wise man tempered by the indulgence of a friend; you have caught a glimpse, through an opera-comique cloud, of a miller's pretty wife with powdered hair, a waist all trimmed with gay ribbons, a light and short skirt, and stockings with gilded clocks; in short, one of those fair young millers' wives whose heart goes pit-a-pat with hautboy accompaniment. But the graces who are ever sporting in your mind sometimes lead it astray; my fair miller is as much like the creature of your imagination as I am like a youthful Colin; her head is adorned with a towering cotton nightcap to which the thickest possible coating of flour fails to restore its primitive color; she wears a coarse woolen petticoat which would abrade the hide of an elephant; in short, it frequently happens to me to confound the miller's wife with the miller himself, after which it is sufficient to add that I am not the least curious to know whether or not her heart goes pit-a-pat. The truth is, that, not knowing how to kill time in your absence, and having no reason to expect you to return before another month; (it's your own fault!), I solicited a mission. The council-general of the department of — had lately, and quite opportunely, expressed officially the wish that a certain ruined abbey, called Rozel Abbey, should be classed among historical monuments. I have been commissioned to investigate closely the candidate's titles. I hastened with all possible speed to the chief town of this artistic department, where I effected my entrance with the important gravity of a man who holds within his hands the life or the death of a monument dear to the country. I made some inquiries at the hotel; great was my mortification when I discovered that no one seemed to suspect that such a thing as Rozel Abbey existed within a circuit of a hundred leagues. I called at the prefecture while still laboring under the effect of this disappointment; the prefect, Valton, whom you know very well, received me with his usual affability; but to the questions I addressed him on the subject of the condition of the ruins which the council seemed so desirous of preserving for the admiration of its constituents, he replied with an absent smile, that his wife, who had visited these ruins on the occasion of an excursion into the country, while she was sojourning on the sea shore, could tell me a great deal more about the ruins than he possibly could himself.

He invited me to dinner, and in the evening, Madame Valton, after the usual struggles of expiring modesty, showed me, in her album, some views of the famous ruins sketched with considerable taste. She became mildly excited while speaking to me of these venerable remains, situated, if she is to be believed, in the midst of an enchanting site, and, above all, particularly well suited for picnics and country excursions. A beseeching and corrupting look terminated her harangue. It seems evident to me that this worthy lady is the only person in the department who takes any real interest in that poor old abbey, and that the conscript fathers of the general council have passed their resolution authorizing an investigation out of pure gallantry. It is impossible for me, however, not to concur in their opinion; the abbey has beautiful eyes; she deserves to be classed—she shall be classed.

My decision was therefore settled, from that moment, but it was still necessary to write it down and back it with some documentary evidence. Unfortunately, the local archives and libraries do not abound in traditions relative to my subject; after two days of conscientious rummaging, I had collected but a few rare and insignificant documents, which may be summed up in these two lines; "Rozel Abbey, in Rozel township, was inhabited from time immemorial by monks, who left it when it fell in ruins."

That is why I resolved to go, without further delay, and ask their secret of these mysterious ruins, and to multiply, if need be, the artifices of my pencil, to make up for the compulsory conciseness of my pen. I left on Wednesday morning for the town of Vitry, which is only two or three leagues distant from the abbey. A Norman coach, complemented with a Norman coachman, jogged me about all day, like an indolent monarch, along the Norman hedges. When night came, I had traveled twelve miles and my coachman had taken twelve meals.

The country is fine, though of a character somewhat uniformly rustic. Under everlasting groves is displayed an opulent and monotonous verdure, in the thickness of which contented-looking oxen ruminate. I can understand my coachman's twelve meals; the idea of eating must occur frequently and almost exclusively to the imagination of any man who spends his life in the midst of this rich nature, the very grass of which gives an appetite.

Toward evening, however, the aspect of the landscape changed; we entered a rolling prairie, quite low, marshy, bare as a Russian steppe, and extending on both sides of the road; the sound of the wheels on the causeway assumed a hollow and vibrating sonority; dark-colored reeds and tall, unhealthy-looking grass covered, as far as the eye could reach, the blackish surface of the marsh. I noticed in the distance, through the deepening twilight, and behind a cloud of rain, two or three horsemen running at full speed, and as if demented, through these boundless spaces; they disappeared at intervals in the depressions of the meadows, and suddenly came to sight again, still galloping with the same frenzy. I could not imagine toward what imaginary goal these equestrian phantoms were thus madly rushing. I took good care not to inquire; mystery is a sweet and sacred thing.

The next morning, I started for the abbey, taking with me in my cabriolet a tall young peasant who had yellow hair, like Ceres. He was a farm-boy who had lived since his birth within a rod of my monument; he had heard me in the morning asking for information in the courtyard of the inn, and had obligingly volunteered to show me the way to the ruins, which were the first thing he had seen on coming into the world. I had no need whatever of a guide; I accepted, nevertheless, the fellow's offer, his officious chattering seeming to promise a well-sustained conversation, in the course of which I hoped to detect some interesting legend; but as soon as he had taken his seat by my side, the rascal became dumb; my questions seemed even, I know not why, to inspire him with a deep mistrust, almost akin to anger. I had to deal with the genius of the ruins, the faithful guardian of their treasures. On the other hand, I had the gratification of taking him home in my carriage; it was apparently all he wished, and he had every reason to be satisfied with my accommodating spirit.

After landing this agreeable companion at his own door, it became necessary for me to alight also; a rocky path, or rather a rude flight of stone steps, winding down the side of a steep declivity, led me to the bottom of a narrow valley which spreads and stretches between a double chain of high wooded hills. A small river flows lazily through it under the shade of alder-bushes, dividing two strips of meadows as fine and velvety as the lawns of a park; it is crossed over by an old bridge with a single arch, which reflects in the placid water the outlines of its graceful ogive. On the right, the hills stand close together in the form of a circus, and seemed to join their verdure-clad curves; on the left, they spread out until they become merged in the deep and somber masses of a vast forest. The valley is thus closed on all sides, and offers a picture of which the calm, the freshness, and the isolation penetrate the soul.

The ruins of the abbey stand with their back against the forest. What remains of the abbey proper is not a great deal. At the entrance of the courtyard, a monumental gateway; a wing of the building, dating from the twelfth century, in which dwell the family of the miller of whom I am the guest; the chapter-hall, remarkable for some elegant arches and a few remnants of mural painting; finally, two or three cells, one of which seems to have been used for the purposes of correction, if I may judge from the solidity of the door and the strength of the bolts. The rest has been torn down, and may be found in fragments among the cottages of the neighborhood. The church, which has almost the proportions of a cathedral, is finely preserved, and produces a marvelous effect. The portal and the apse have alone disappeared; the whole interior architecture, the copings, the tall columns, are intact and as if built yesterday. There, it seems, that an artist must have presided over the work of destruction; a masterly stroke of the pick-ax has opened at the two extremities of the church, where stood the portal and where stood the altar, two gigantic bays, so that, from the threshold of the edifice, the eye plunges into the forest beyond as through a deep triumphal arch. In this solitary spot the effect is unexpected and solemn. I was delighted with it. "Monsieur," I said to the miller, who, since my arrival, had been watching my every step from a distance with that fierce mistrust which is a peculiarity of this part of the country, "I have been requested to examine and to sketch these ruins. That work will require several days; could you not spare me a daily trip from the town to the abbey and back, by furnishing me with such accommodations as you can, for a week or two?"

The miller, a thorough Norman, examined me from head to foot without answering, like a man who knows that silence is of gold; he measured me, he gauged me, he weighed me, and finally, opening his flour-coated lips, he called his wife. The latter appeared at once upon the threshold of the chapter-hall, converted into a cow-pen, and I had to repeat my request to her. She examined me in her turn, but not at such great length as her husband, and, with the superior scent of her sex, her conclusion was, as I had the right to expect, that of the *præses* in the *Malade Imaginaire*: "*Dignus es intrare.*" The miller, who saw what turn things were taking, lifted his cap and treated me to a smile. I must add that these excellent people, once the ice was broken, tried in every way to compensate me, by a thousand eager attentions, for the excessive caution of their reception. They wished to give up to me their own room, adorned with the Adventures of Telemachus, but I preferred—as Mentor would have done—a cell of austere nudity, of which the window, with small, lozenge-shaped panes, opens on the ruined portal of the church and the horizon of the forest.

Had I been a few years younger, I would have enjoyed keenly this poetic installation; but I am turning gray, friend Paul, or at least I fear so, though I try still to attribute to a mere effect of light the doubtful shades that dot my beard under the rays of the noonday sun. Nevertheless, if my reverie has changed its object, it still lasts, and still has its charms for me. My poetic feeling has become modified and, I think, more elevated. The image of a woman is no longer the indispensable element of my dreams; my heart, peaceful now, and striving to become still more so, is gradually withdrawing from the field of my mind's labors. I cannot, I confess, find enough pleasure in the pure and dry meditations of the intellect; my imagination must speak first and set my brain in motion, for I was born romantic, and romantic I shall die; and all that can be asked of me, all I can obtain of myself, at an age when propriety already commands gravity, is to build romances without love.

Up to this time, ennui has spared me in my solitude. Shall I confess to you that I even experience in it a singular feeling of contentment? It seems as though I were a thousand leagues away from the things of the world, and that there is a sort of truce and respite in the miserable routine of my existence, at once so agitated and so commonplace. I relish my complete independence with the naïve joy of a twelve-year-old Robinson Crusoe. I sketch when I feel like it; the rest of the time, I walk here and there at random, being careful only never to go beyond the bounds of the sacred valley. I sit down upon the parapet of the bridge, and I watch the running water; I go on voyages of discovery among the ruins; I dive into the underground vaults; I scale the shattered steps of the belfry, and being unable to come down again the same way, I remain astride a gargoyle, cutting a rather sorry figure, until the miller brings me a ladder. I wander at night through the forest, and I see deer running by in the moonlight. All these things have a soothing effect on my mind, and produce the effect of child's dream in middle age.

Your letter dated from Cologne, and which was forwarded to me here according to my instructions, has alone disturbed my beatitude. I console myself with some difficulty for having left Paris almost on the eve of your return. May Heaven confound your whims and your want of decision! All I can do now, is to hurry my work; but where shall I find the historical documents I still need? I am seriously anxious to save these ruins. There is here a rare landscape, a valuable picture, which it would be sheer vandalism to allow to perish.

And then, I admire the old monks! I wish to offer up to their departed shades this homage of my sympathy. Yes, had I lived some thousand years ago, I would certainly have sought among them the repose of the cloister while waiting for the peace of heaven. What existence could have suited me better? Free from the cares of this world, and assured of the other, free from any agitations of the heart or the mind, I would have placidly written simple legends which I would have been credulous enough to believe; I would have unraveled with intense curiosity some unknown manuscripts, and discovered with tears of joy the Iliad or the Æneid; I would have sketched imaginary cathedrals; I would have heated alembics—and perhaps have invented gunpowder; which is by no means the best thing I might have done.

Come! 'tis midnight; brother, we must sleep!

Postscriptum.—There are ghosts! I was closing this letter, my dear friend, in the midst of a solemn silence, when suddenly my ears were filled with mysterious and confused sounds that seemed to come from the outside, and among which I thought I could distinguish the buzzing murmur of a large crowd. I approached, quite surprised, the window of my cell, and I could not exactly tell you the nature of the emotion I felt on discovering the ruins of the church illuminated with a resplendent blaze; the vast portal and the yawning ogives cast floods of light far as the distant woods. It was not, it could not be, an accidental conflagration. Besides, I could see, through the stone trefoils, shadows of superhuman size flitting through the nave, apparently performing, with a sort of rhythm, some mysterious ceremony. I threw my window abruptly open; at the same instant, a loud blast broke forth in the ruins, and rang again through all the echoes of the valley; after which, I saw issuing from the church a double file of horsemen bearing torches and blowing horns, some dressed in red, others draped in black, with plumes waving over their heads. This strange procession followed, still in the same order, amid the same dazzling light and the same clangor of trumpets, the shaded path that skirts the edge of the meadows. Having reached the little bridge, it stopped; I saw the torches rise, wave, and cast showers of sparks; the horns sounded a weird and prolonged blast; then suddenly every light disappeared, every noise ceased, and the valley was again wrapped in the darkness and the deep silence of the night. That is what I saw and heard. You who have just arrived from Germany, did you meet the Black Huntsman? No? Hang yourself, then!

CHAPTER II.

Hunting a Wild Man.

16th September.

The forest which once formed part of the demesnes of the abbey, now belongs to a wealthy landed proprietor of the district, the Marquis de Malouet, a lineal descendant of Nimrod, whose chateau seems to be the social center of the district. There are almost daily at this season grand hunts in the forest; yesterday, the party ended with a supper on the grass, and afterward a ride home by torchlight. I felt very much disposed to strangle the honest miller, who gave me this morning, in vulgar language, this explanation of my midnight ballad.

There is the world, then, invading with all its pomp my beloved solitude. I curse it, Paul, with all the bitterness of my heart. I became indebted to it, last night, it is true, for a fantastic apparition that both charmed and delighted me; but I am also indebted to it today for a ridiculous adventure which I am the only one not to laugh at, for I was its unlucky hero.

I was but little disposed to work this morning; I went on sketching, however, until noon, but had to give it up then; my head was heavy, I felt dull and disagreeable, I had a vague presentiment of something fatal in the air. I returned for a moment to the mill to get rid of my traps; I quarreled, to her surprise and grief, with the miller's wife, on the subject of I know not what cruelly indigenous mess she had served me for breakfast; I scolded the good woman's two children because they were touching my pencils; finally, I administered a vigorous kick to the housedog, accompanied with the celebrated formula: "Judge whether you had done anything to me!"

Rather dissatisfied with myself, as you may imagine, after these three mean little tricks, I directed my steps toward the forest, in order to hide as much as possible from the light of the day. I walked about for nearly an hour without being able to shake off the prophetic melancholy that oppressed me. Perceiving at last, on the edge of one of the avenues that traverse the forest, and under the dense shade of some beech-trees, a thick bed of moss, I stretched myself upon it, together with my remorse, and it was not long before I fell into a sound sleep. Mon Dieu! why was it not the sleep of death?

I have no idea how long I had been asleep, when I was suddenly awakened by a certain concussion of the soil in my immediate vicinity; I jumped abruptly to my feet, and I saw, within five steps of me, on the road, a young lady on horseback. My unexpected apparition had somewhat frightened the horse, who had shied with some violence. The fair equestrian, who had not yet noticed me, was talking to him and trying to quiet him. She appeared to be pretty, slender, elegant. I caught a rapid glimpse of blond hair, eyebrows of a darker shade, keen eyes, a bold expression of countenance, and a felt hat with blue feathers, set over one ear in rather too rakish a style. For the better understanding of what is about to follow, you should know that I was attired in a tourist's blouse stained with red ochre; besides, I must have had that haggard look and startled expression which impart to one rudely snatched from sleep a countenance at once comical and alarming. Add to all this, my hair in utter disorder, my beard strewn with dead leaves, and you will have no difficulty in understanding the terror that suddenly overpowered the young huntress at the first glance she cast upon me; she uttered a feeble cry, and wheeling her horse around, she fled at full gallop.

It was impossible for me to mistake the nature of the impression I had just produced; there was nothing flattering about it. However, I am thirty-five years of age, and the more or less kindly glance of a woman is no longer sufficient to disturb the serenity of my soul. I followed with a smiling look the flying Amazon. At the extremity of the avenue in which I had just failed to make her conquest, she turned abruptly to the left, to go and take a parallel road. I only had to cross the adjoining thicket to see her overtake a cavalcade composed of ten or twelve persons, who seemed to be waiting for her, and to whom she shouted from a distance, in a broken voice:

"Gentlemen! gentlemen! a wild man! there is a wild man in the forest!"

My interest being highly excited by this beginning, I settle myself comfortably behind a thick bush, with eye and ear equally attentive. They crowd around the lady; it is supposed at first that she is jesting, but her emotion is too serious to have been causeless. She saw, distinctly saw, not exactly a savage, perhaps, but a man in rags, whose tattered blouse seemed covered with blood, whose face, hands, and whole person were repulsively filthy, whose beard was frightful, and whose eyes half protruded from their sockets; in short, an individual, by the side of whom the most atrocious of Salvator Rosa's brigands would be as one of Watteau's shepherds. Never did a man's vanity enjoy such a treat! This charming person added that I had threatened her, and that I had jumped at her horse's bridle like the specter of the forest of Mans.[1]

The response to this marvelous story is a general and enthusiastic shout:

"Let us chase him! let us surround him! let us track him! hip, hip, hurrah!"—whereupon the whole cavalry force starts off at a gallop in the direction given by the amiable story teller.

I had, to all appearances, but to remain quietly ensconced in my hiding place in order to completely foil the hunters who were going in search of me in the avenue where I had met the beautiful Amazon. Unfortunately, I had the unlucky idea, for greater safety, of making my way into the opposite thicket. As I was cautiously crossing the open space, a wild shout of joy informs me that I have been discovered; at the same time, I see the whole squadron wheeling about and coming down upon me like a torrent. There remained but one reasonable course for me to pursue; it was to stop, to affect the surprise of a quiet stroller disturbed in his walk, and to disconcert my assailants by an attitude at once simple and dignified; but, seized with a foolish shame which it is easier to conceive than to explain—convinced, moreover, that a vigorous effort would be sufficient to rid me of this importunate pursuit and to spare me the annoyance of an explanation—I commit the error—the ever deplorable error—of hurrying on faster, or rather, to be frank with you, of running away as fast as my legs would carry me. I cross the road like a hare, I penetrate

---

1   Charles VI., King of France, became demented in consequence of his
     horse being stopped, during a hunt in the forest of Mans, by what
     seemed to him a supernatural being.—(Trans.)

into the thicket, greeted on my passage with a volley of joyous clamors. From that moment my fate was sealed; all honorable explanation became impossible for me; I had ostensibly accepted the struggle with its most extreme chances.

However, I still possessed a certain presence of mind, and while tearing furiously through the brambles, I soothed myself with comforting reflections. Once separated from my persecutors by the whole depth of a thicket inaccessible to cavalry, it would be an easy matter to gain a sufficient advance upon them to be able to laugh at their fruitless search. This last illusion vanished when, on reaching the limit of the covered space, I discovered that the cursed troop had divided into two squads, who were both waiting for me at the outlet. At the sight of me, a fresh storm of shouts and laughter broke forth, and the hunting horns sounded in all directions. I became dizzy; I felt the forest whirling around me; I rushed into the first path that offered itself to me, and my flight assumed the character of a hopeless rout.

The implacable legion of hunters and huntresses did not fail to start on my heels with renewed ardor and stupid mirth. I still recognized at their head the lady with the waving blue plume, who distinguished herself by her peculiar animosity, and upon whom I invoked with all my heart the most serious accidents to which equestrianism may be subject. It was she who encouraged her odious accomplices, when I had succeeded for a moment in eluding the pursuit; she discovered me with infernal keen-sightedness, pointed me out with the tip of her whip, and broke into a barbarous laugh whenever she saw me resume my race through the bushes, blowing, panting, desperate, absurd. I ran thus during a space of time of which I am unable to form any estimate, accomplishing unprecedented feats of gymnastics, tearing through the thorny brambles, sinking into the miry spots, leaping over the ditches, bounding upon my feet with the elasticity of a panther, galloping to the devil, without reason, without object, and without any other hope but that of seeing the earth open beneath my feet.

At last, and surely by chance—for I had long since lost all topographical notions—I discovered the ruins just ahead of me; with a last effort, I cleared the open space that separates them from the forest; I ran through the church as if I had been excommunicated, and I arrived panting before the door of the mill. The miller and his wife were standing on the threshold, attracted, doubtless, by the noise of the cavalcade that was following close on my heels; they looked at me with an expression of stupor; I tried in vain to find a few words of explanation to cast to them as I ran by, and after incredible efforts of intelligence, I was only able to murmur in a silly tone: "If any one asks for me, say I am not in!" Then I cleared in three jumps the stairs leading to my cell, and I sank upon my bed in a state of complete prostration.

In the meantime, Paul, the hunting-party were crowding tumultuously into the courtyard of the abbey; I could hear the stamping of the horses' feet, the voices of the riders, and even the sound of their boots on the flagging, which proved that some of them had alighted and were threatening me with a last assault. I started up with a gesture of rage, and I glanced at my pistols. Fortunately, after a few minutes' conversation with the miller, the hunters withdrew, not without giving me to understand that, if they had formed a better opinion of my character, they went away with a most amusing idea of the eccentricity of my disposition.

Such is, my dear friend, a faithful historical account of that unlucky day, during which I covered myself frankly, and from head to foot, with a species of humiliation to which any Frenchman would prefer that of crime. I have, at this moment, the satisfaction of knowing that I am in a neighboring chateau, in the midst of a gathering of brilliant men and lovely young women, an inexhaustible subject for jokes. I feel, moreover, since my flank movement (as it is customary in war to call precipitate retreats), that I have lost something of my dignity in my own eyes, and I cannot conceal to myself, besides, that I am far from enjoying the same consideration on the part of my rustic hosts.

In presence of a situation so seriously compromised, it became necessary to hold council; after a brief deliberation, I rejected far, far from me, as puerile and pusillanimous, the project suggested to me by my vanity at bay, that of giving up my lodgings, and even of leaving the district entirely. I made up my mind to pursue philosophically the course of my labors and my pleasures, to show a soul superior to circumstances, and in short, to give to the Amazons, the centaurs, and the millers the fine spectacle of the wise man in adversity.

CHAPTER III.

The Marquis de Malouet.

Malouet, *20th September.*

I have just received your letter. You belong to the true breed of Monomotapa friends, Paul. But what puerility! And such is the case of your sudden return! A trifle, a silly nightmare which for two successive nights caused you to hear the sound of my voice calling on you for help! Ah! bitter fruits of the wretched German cuisine! Really, Paul, you are foolish! And yet, you tell me things that move me to tears. I cannot answer you as I would like to. My heart is tender, but my speech is dry. I have never been able to tell any one, "I love you!" There is a jealous fiend who checks on my lips every word of affection, and imparts to it a tone of irony. But, thank God, you know me!

It seems that I make you laugh while you make me weep! Well, I am glad of it. Yes, my noble adventure in the forest has had a sequel, and a sequel with which I might very well have dispensed. All the misfortunes which you felt were threatening me have actually happened to me; rest easy, therefore.

The day following this fatal day, I began by reconquering the esteem of my hosts at the mill, by relating to them good-naturedly the most piquant episodes of my famous race. I saw them beaming as they heard the narrative; the woman in particular was writhing in atrocious convulsions, and with formidable stretches of her jaws. I have never seen anything so hideous, in all my life, as this coarse, cowherd's joy!

As a testimonial of the complete restoration of his sympathy, the miller asked me if I was fond of hunting, took down from a hook over his mantelpiece a long, rusty tube, that made me think of Leather Stocking's rifle, and laid it into my hands, while boasting of the murderous qualities of that instrument. I acknowledged his kindness with an outward appearance of lively satisfaction, never having had the heart to undeceive people who think they are doing something to please me, and I started for the woods that cover the hillsides, carrying like a lance that venerable weapon, which seemed indeed to me of the most dangerous kind. I went to take a seat on the heather, and I carefully laid down the long gun by me; then I amused myself driving away, by throwing stones at them, the young rabbits that ventured imprudently in the vicinity of an engine of war for the effects of which I could not be responsible. Thanks to these precautions, for over an hour that this hunt lasted, no accident happened either to the game or to myself.

To speak candidly, I was rather glad to allow the hour to pass when the hunting party from the chateau are in the habit of taking the field, not caring very much, through a remnant of vain glory, to find myself on their passage that day. Toward two o'clock in the afternoon, I left my seat of mint and wild thyme, satisfied that I had henceforth no unpleasant encounter to apprehend. I handed the blunderbuss to the miller, who seemed somewhat surprised to see me empty-handed, and more so, probably, to see me alive still. I went to take a stand opposite the portal, and I undertook to finish a general view of the ruin, a watercolor, which, I feel, is certain to secure the approbation of the minister.

I was deeply absorbed in my work, when I suddenly fancied I could hear more distinctly than usual that sound of running horses which, since my misadventure, was forever haunting my ears. I turned around sharply, and I discovered the enemy within two hundred paces of me. This time, he was attired in plain clothes, being apparently equipped for an ordinary ride; he had obtained, since the previous day, several recruits of both sexes, and now really formed an imposing body. Though long prepared for such an occurrence, I could not help feeling a certain discomfort, and I secretly cursed those indefatigable idlers. Nevertheless, the thought of retreating never occurred to me; I had lost all taste for flight for the rest of my days.

As the cavalcade drew nearer, I could hear smothered laughter and whisperings, the subject of which was but too evident to me. I must confess that a spark of anger was beginning to burn in my heart, and while going on with my work with an appearance of unabated interest, and indulging in admiring motions of the head before my watercolor, I was lending to the scene going on behind me a somber and vigilant attention. However, the first intention of the party seemed to be to spare my misfortune; instead of following the path by the side of which I was established, and which was the shortest way to the ruins, they turned aside toward the right, and filed by in silence. One alone among them, falling out of the main group, came rapidly in my direction, and stopped within ten steps of my studio; though my face was bent over my drawing, I felt, by that strange intuition which every one knows, a human look fixed upon me. I raised my eyes with an air of indifference, dropping them again almost immediately; that rapid gesture had been sufficient to enable me to recognize in that indiscreet observer the young lady with the blue feathers, the original cause of all my mishaps. She was there, boldly seated on her horse, her chin raised, her eyes half closed, examining me from head to foot with admirable insolence. I had thought it best at first, out of respect for her sex, to abandon myself without resistance to her impertinent curiosity; but after a few seconds, as she manifested no intention of putting an end to her proceedings, I lost patience, and raising my head more openly, I fixed my eyes upon her with polite gravity, but persistent steadiness. She blushed; seeing which, I bowed. She returned me a slight inclination of the head, and moving off at a canter, she disappeared under the vault of the old church. I thus remained master of the field, keenly relishing the triumph of fascination I had just obtained over that little person, whom there certainly was considerable merit in putting out of countenance.

The ride through the forest lasted some twenty minutes, and I soon beheld the brilliant fantasia debouching pell-mell from the portal. I feigned again a profound abstraction; but this time again, one of the riders left the company and advanced toward me; he was a man of tall stature, who wore a blue frock-coat, buttoned up to his chin, in military style. He was marching so straight upon my little establishment, that I could not help supposing he intended passing right over it for the amusement of the ladies. I was therefore watching him with a furtive but wide awake glance, when I had the satisfaction of seeing him stop within three steps of my camp-stool, and removing his hat.

"Monsieur," he said, in a full and frank tone of voice, "will you permit me to look at your drawing?"

I returned his salutation, nodded in token of acquiescence, and went on with my work. After a moment of silent contemplation, the unknown equestrian, apparently yielding to the violence of his impressions, allowed a few laudatory epithets to escape him; then, resuming his direct allocution:

"Monsieur," he said, "allow me to return thanks to your talent; we shall be indebted to it, I feel quite sure, for the preservation of these ruins, which are the ornament of our district."

I abandoned at once my reserve, which could no longer be anything but childish sulkiness, and I replied, as I thought I should, that he was appreciating with too much indulgence a mere amateur's sketch; that I certainly had the greatest desire of saving these beautiful ruins, but that the most important part of my work threatened to remain quite insignificant, for want of historical information which I had vainly tried to find in the archives of the county-seat.

"Parbleu, monsieur," rejoined the horseman, "you please me greatly. I have in my library a large proportion of the archives of the abbey. Come and consult them at your leisure. I shall feel grateful to you for doing so."

I thanked him with some embarrassment. I regretted not to have known it sooner. I feared being recalled to Paris by a letter which I was expecting this very day. Nevertheless, I had risen to make this answer, the ill grace of which I strove to attenuate by the courteousness of my attitude. At the same time, I formed a clearer idea of my interlocutor; he was a handsome old man, with broad shoulders, who seemed to carry with ease the weight of some sixty winters, and whose bright blue eyes expressed the kindliest good feeling.

"Come! come!" he exclaimed, "let us speak frankly. You feel some repugnance at mingling with that band of harebrained scamps you see yonder, and whom I tried in vain yesterday to keep out of a silly affair, for which I now beg to tender you my sincere apologies. My name is the Marquis de Malouet, sir. After all, you went off with the honors of the day. They wished to see you; you did not wish to be seen. You carried your point. What else can you ask?"

I could not help laughing on hearing such a favorable interpretation of my unlucky scrape.

"You laugh!" rejoined the old marquis; "bravo! we'll soon come to an understanding, then. Now, what's to prevent your coming to spend a few days at my house? My wife has requested me to invite you; she has heard in detail all your annoyances of yesterday. She has an angel's disposition, my wife. She is no longer young, always ill; a mere breath; but she is an angel. I'll locate you in the library—you'll live like a hermit, if you like. Mon Dieu! I see it all, I tell you; these madcaps of mine frighten you; you are a serious man; I know all about that sort of disposition! Well! you'll find congenial company—my wife is full of sense; I am no fool myself. I am fond of exercise; in fact, it is indispensable to my health—but you must not take me for a brute! The devil! not at all! I'll astonish you. You must be fond of whist; we'll have a game together; you must like to live well—delicately, I mean, as it is proper and suitable for a man of taste and intelligence. Well! since you appreciate good living, I am your man; I have an excellent cook. I may even say that I have two for the present; one coming in and the other going out; it is a conjunction; the result is, a contest of skill, an academic tourney, of which you will assist me in adjudging the prize! Come! sir," he added, laughing ingenuously at his own chattering, "it's settled, isn't it? I'm going to carry you off."

Happy Paul, thrice happy is the man who can say No! Alone, he is really master of his time, of his fortune, and of his honor. One should be able to say No! even to a beggar, even to a woman, even to an amiable old man, under penalty of surrendering at hazard his charity, his dignity, and his independence. For want of a manly No, how much misery, how many downfalls, how many crimes since Adam!

While I was considering in my own mind the invitation which had just been extended to me, these thoughts crowded in my brain; I recognized their profound wisdom, and I said Yes! Fatal word, through which I lost my paradise, exchanging a retreat wholly to my taste—peaceful, laborious, romantic, and free—for the stiffness of a residence where society displays all the fury of its insipid dissipations.

I demanded the necessary time for effecting my removal, and Monsieur de Malouet left me, after grasping my hand cordially, declaring that he was extremely pleased with me, and that he was going to stimulate his two cooks to give me a triumphant reception. "I am going," he said in conclusion, "to announce to them an artist, a poet: that'll work up their imagination."

Toward five o'clock, two valets from the chateau came to take charge of my light baggage, and to advise me that a carriage was waiting for me on top of the hills. I bade farewell to my cell; I thanked my hosts; and I kissed their little urchins, all besmeared and ill-kempt as they were. These kind people seemed to see me going with regret. I felt, myself, an extraordinary and unaccountable sadness. I know not what strange sentiment attached me to that valley, but I left it with an aching heart, as one leaves his native country.

More tomorrow, Paul, for I am exhausted.

CHAPTER IV.

The Little Countess.

26th September.

The chateau of Malouet is a massive and rather vulgar construction, which dates some one hundred years back. Fine avenues, a court of honor of a handsome style, and an ancient park impart to it, however, an aspect truly seigneurial.

The old marquis came to receive me at the foot of the stoop, passed his arm under mine, and after leading me through a long maze of corridors, introduced me into a vast drawing-room, where almost complete obscurity prevailed; I could only vaguely distinguish, by the intermittent blaze of the hearth, some twenty persons of both sexes, scattered here and there in small groups. Thanks to this blessed twilight, I effected safely my entrance, which had at a distance offered itself to my imagination, under a solemn and somewhat alarming light. I had barely time to receive the compliment of welcome which Madame de Malouet addressed me in a feeble but penetrating voice. She took my arm almost at once to pass into the dining-room, having resolved, it appears, to refuse no mark of consideration to a pedestrian of such surprising agility.

Once at the table and in the bright light, I was not long in discovering that my feats of the previous day had by no means been forgotten, and that I was the center of general attention; but I stood bravely this crossfire of curious and ironical glances, intrenched on the one hand behind a mountain of flowers that ornamented the center of the table, and on the other assisted in my defensive position by the ingenious kindness of my neighbor. Madame de Malouet is one of those rare old women whom superior strength of mind or great purity of soul has preserved against despair at the fatal hour of the fortieth year, and who have saved from the wreck of their youth a single waif, itself a supreme charm, grace. Small, frail, her face pale and withered from the effects of habitual suffering, she justifies exactly her husband's expression: "She is a breath, a breath that exhales intelligence and good-nature!" Not a shadow of any pretension unbecoming her age, an exquisite care of her person without the faintest trace of coquetry, a complete oblivion of her departed youth, a sort of bashfulness at being old, and a touching desire, not to please, but to be forgiven; such is my adorable marquise. She has traveled much, read much, and knows Paris well. I roamed with her through one of those rapid conversations in which two minds whirl and for the first time seek to become acquainted, rambling from one pole to the other, touching lightly upon all things, disputing gayly, and happy to agree.

Monsieur de Malouet seized the opportunity of the removal of the colossal dish that separated us, to ascertain the condition of my relations with his wife. He seemed satisfied at our evident good intelligence, and raising his sonorous and cordial voice:

"Monsieur," he said to me, "I have spoken to you of my two rival cooks; now is the time to justify the reputation of high discernment which I have attributed to you in the minds of these artists.

"Alas! I am about to lose the oldest, and without doubt the most skillful, of these masters—the illustrious Jean Rostain. It was he, sir, who, on his arrival from Paris, two years ago, made this remarkable speech to me: 'A man of taste, Monsieur le Marquis, can no longer live in Paris; they practice there now, a certain romantic style of cooking which will lead us Heaven knows where!' In short, sir, Rostain is a classic; this singular man has an opinion of his own! Well! you have just tasted in succession two *entremets* dishes of which cream forms the essential foundation; according to my idea, these dishes are both a success; but Rostain's work has struck me as greatly superior. Ah, ah! sir, I am curious to know if you can of your own accord and upon that simple indication, assign to each tree its fruit, and render unto Cæsar what belongs to Cæsar. Ah, ah, let us see if you can!"

I cast a furtive glance at the remnants of the two dishes to which the marquis had just called my attention, and I had no hesitation in designating as "classic" the one that was surmounted with a temple of cupid, and a figure of that god in polychromatic pastry.

"A hit!" exclaimed the marquis. "Bravo! Rostain shall hear of it, and his heart will rejoice. Ah! monsieur, why has it not been my good fortune to receive you in my house a few days sooner? I might perhaps have kept Rostain, or, to speak more truly, Rostain might perhaps have kept me; for I cannot conceal the fact, gentlemen hunters, that you are not in the good graces of the old *chef*, and I am not far from attributing his departure with whatever pretexts he may choose to color it, to the annoyance he feels at your complete indifference. Thinking it might be agreeable to him, I informed him, a few weeks ago, that our hunting-meetings were about to secure him a concourse of connoisseurs worthy of his talents."

"Monsiuer le Marquis will excuse me," replied Rostain with a melancholy smile, "if I do not share his illusions; in the first place, the hunter devours and does not eat; he brings to the table the stomach of a man just saved from shipwreck, *iratum ventrem*, as Horace says, and swallows up without choice and without reflection, *gulæ parens*, the most serious productions of an artist; in the second place, the violent exercise of the chase has developed in such guests an inordinate thirst, which they generally slake without moderation. Now, Monsieur le Marquis is not ignorant of the opinion of the ancients on the excessive use of wine during meals; it blunts the taste—*ersurdant vina palatum!* Nevertheless, Monsieur le Marquis may rest assured that I shall labor to please his guests with my usual conscientiousness, though with the painful certainty of not being understood."

After uttering these words, Rostain draped himself in his toga, cast to heaven the look of an unappreciated genius, and left my study.

"I would have thought," I said to the marquis, "that you would have spared no sacrifice to retain that great man."

"You judge me correctly, sir," replied Monsieur de Malouet; "but you'll see that he carried me to the very limits of impossibility. Precisely a week ago, Monsieur Rostain, having solicited a private audience, announced to me that he found himself under the painful necessity of leaving my service. 'Heavens! Monsieur Rostain to leave my service! And where do you expect to go?' 'To Paris.' 'What! to Paris! But you had shaken upon the great Babylon the dust of your sandals! The decadence of taste, the increasing development of the romantic cuisine! Such are your own words, Rostain!' He replied: 'Doubtless, Monsieur le Marquis; but provincial life has bitter trials which I had not foreseen!' I offered him fabulous wages; he refused. 'Come, my good fellow, what is the matter? Ah! I see, you don't like the scullery maid; she disturbs your meditations by her vulgar songs; very well, consider her dismissed! That is not enough? Is it Antoine, then, who is objectionable? I'll discharge him! Is it the coachman? I'll send him away!' In short, I offered him, gentlemen, the whole household as a holocaust. But, at all these prodigious concessions, the old *chef* shook his head with indifference. But finally, I exclaimed, 'in the name of Heaven, Monsieur Rostain, do explain!' 'Mon Dieu! Monsieur le Marquis,' then said Jean Rostain, 'I must confess to you that it is impossible for me to live in a place where I find no one to play a game of billiards with me!' *Ma foi!* it was a little too much!" added the marquis, with a cheerful good-nature.

"I could not really offer to play billiards with him myself! I had to submit. I wrote at once to Paris, and last evening a young cook arrived, who wears a mustache and gave his name as Jacquemart (of Bordeaux). The classic Rostain, in a sublime impulse of artistic pride, volunteered to assist Monsieur Jacquemart (of Bordeaux) in his first effort, and that's how, gentlemen, I was able today to serve this great eclectic dinner, of which, I fear, we will alone, monsieur and myself, have appreciated the mysterious beauties."

Monsieur de Malouet rose from the table as he was concluding the story of Rostain's epic. After coffee, I followed the smokers into the garden. The evening was magnificent. The marquis led me away along the main avenue, the fine sand of which sparkled in the moonlight between the dense shadows of the tall chestnuts. While talking with apparent carelessness, he submitted me to a sort of examination upon a variety of subjects, as if to make sure that I was worthy of the interest he had so gratuitously manifested toward me up to this time. We were far from agreeing on all points; but, gifted both with sincerity and good-nature, we found almost as much pleasure in arguing as we did in agreeing. That epicurean is a thinker; his thought, always generously inclined, has assumed, in the solitude where it has developed itself, a peculiar and paradoxical turn. I wish I could give you an idea of it.

As we were returning to the chateau, we heard a great noise of voices and laughter, and we saw at the foot of the stoop some ten or twelve young men who were jumping and bounding, as if trying to reach, without the help of the steps, the platform that crowns the double staircase. We were enabled to understand the explanation of these passionate gymnastics as soon as the light of the moon enabled us to distinguish a white dress on the platform. It was evidently a tournament of which the white dress was to crown the victor. The young lady (had she not been young, they would not have jumped so high) was leaning over the balustrade, exposing boldly to the dew of an autumn night, and to the kisses of Diana, her flower-wreathed head and her bare shoulders; she was slightly stooping down, and held out to the competitors an object somewhat difficult to discern at a distance; it was a slender cigarette, the delicate handiwork of her white fingers and her rosy nails. Although there was nothing in the sight that was not charming, Monsieur de Malouet probably found in it something he did not like, for his tone of cheerful good-humor became suddenly shaded with a perceptible tint of annoyance, when he murmured:

"There it is again! I was sure of it! It is the Little Countess!"

It is hardly necessary for me to add that I had recognized, in the Little Countess, my Amazon with the blue plume, who, with or without plume, seems to have always the same disposition. She recognized me perfectly also, on her side, as you'll see directly. At the moment when we were reaching, Monsieur Malouet and myself, the top of the stoop, leaving the rival pretenders to vie and struggle with increasing ardor, the little countess, intimidated perhaps by the presence of the marquis, resolved to put an end to the scene, and thrust abruptly her cigarette into my hand, saying:

"Here! it's for you! After all, you jump better than any of them."

And she disappeared after this parting shaft, which possessed the double advantage of hitting at once both the victor and the vanquished.

This was, so far as I am concerned, the last noticeable episode of the evening. After a game or two of whist, I pretended a little fatigue, and Monsieur de Malouet had the kindness to escort me in person to a pretty little room, hung with chintz and contiguous to the library. I was disturbed during part of the night by the monotonous sound of the piano and the rumbling noise of the carriages, indications of civilization which made me regret more bitterly than ever my poor Thebais.

CHAPTER V.

A Denunciation Overheard.

28th September.

I had the satisfaction of discovering in the library of the marquis the historical documents I needed. They form, indeed, a part of the ancient archives of the abbey, and have a special interest for the family of Malouet. It was one William Malouet, a very noble man and a knight, who, about the middle of the twelfth century, with the consent of messieurs his sons, Hughes, Foulgues, John, and Thomas, restored the church and founded the abbey in favor of the order of the Benedictine monks, and for the salvation of his soul and of the souls of his ancestors, granting unto the congregation, among other dues and privileges, the fee-simple of the lands of the abbey, the tithe of all its revenues, half the wool of its flocks, three loads of wax to be received every year at Mount Saint-Michel-on-the-sea; then the river, the moors, the woods, and the mill, *et molendinum in eodem situ.* I took pleasure in following through the wretched latin of the time the description of this familiar landscape. It has not changed.

The foundation charter bears date 1145. Subsequent charters show that the abbey of Rozel was in possession, in the thirteenth century, of a sort of patriarchate over all the institutions of the order of Saint Benedict that were then in existence in the province of Normandy. A general chapter of the order was held there every year, presided over by the Abbot of Rozel, and at which some ten or a dozen other convents were represented by their highest dignitaries. The discipline, the labors, the temporal and spiritual management of all the Benedictines of the province were here controlled and reformed with a severity which the minutes of these little councils attest in the noblest terms. These scenes replete with dignity, took place in that Capitulary Hall now so shamefully defiled.

Aside from the archives, this library is very rich, and this is apt to divert attention. Moreover, the vortex of worldly dissipation that rages in the chateau is not without occasionally doing some prejudice to my independence. Finally, my worthy hosts frequently take away with one hand the liberty they have granted me with the other; like many persons of the world, they have not a very clear idea of the degree of connected occupation which deserves the name of work, and an hour or two of reading appears to them the utmost extent of labor that a man can bear in a day.

"Consider yourself wholly free," Monsieur le Malouet tells me every morning; "go up to your hermitage; work at your ease."

An hour later he is knocking at my door:

"Well! are we hard at work?"

"Why, yes, I am beginning to get into it."

"What! the duse! You have been at it more than two hours! You are killing yourself, my friend. However, you are free. By the way, my wife is in the parlor; when you have done you'll go and keep her company, won't you?"

"Most undoubtdedly I will."

"But only when you have entirely done, of course."

And, he goes off for a hunt or a ride by the seaside. As to myself, preoccupied with the idea than I am expected, and satisfied that I shall be unable to do any further work of value, I soon resolve to go and join Madame de Malouet, whom I find deeply engaged in conversation with the parish priest, or with Jacquemart (of Bordeaux). She has disturbed me, I am in her way, and we smile pleasantly to each other.

Such is the manner in which the middle of the day usually passes off.

In the morning, I ride on horseback with the marquis, who is kind enough to spare me the crowd and tumult of the general riding-parties. In the evening, I take a hand at whist, then I chat a while with the ladies, and I try my best to cast off at their feet my bear's skin and reputation; for I dislike to display any eccentricity of my own, this one rather more so than any other. There is in a grave disposition, when carried to the point of stiffness and ill-grace toward women, something coarsely pedantic, that is unbecoming in great talents and ridiculous in lesser ones. I retire afterward, and I work rather late in the library. That's the best of my day.

The society at the chateau is usually made up of the marquis' guests, who are always numerous at this season, and of a few persons of the neighborhood. The object of these entertainments on a grand scale is, above all, to celebrate the visit of Monsieur de Malouet's only daughter, who comes every year to spend the autumn with her family. She is a person of statuesque beauty, who amuses herself with queenly dignity, and who communicates with ordinary mortals by means of contemptuous monosyllables uttered in a deep bass voice. She married, some twelve years ago, an Englishman, a member of the diplomatic corps, Lord A——, a personage equally handsome and impassive as herself. He addresses at intervals to his wife an English monosyllable, to which the latter replies imperturbably with a French monosyllable. Nevertheless, three little lords, worthy the pencil of Lawrence, who strut majestically around this Olympian couple, attest between the two nations a secret intelligence which escapes the vulgar observer.

A scarcely less remarkable couple comes over to us daily from a neighboring chateau. The husband is one Monsiuer de Breuilly, formerly an officer in King Charles X's bodyguards, and a bosom friend of the marquis. He is a very lively old man, still quite fine-looking, and wearing over close-cropped gray hair a hat too small for his head. He has an odd, though perhaps natural, way of scanning his words, and of speaking with a degree of deliberation that seems affected. He would be quite pleasant, however, were it not that his mind is constantly tortured by an ardent jealousy, and by a no less ardent apprehension of betraying his weakness, which, nevertheless, is a glaring and obvious fact to every one. It is difficult to understand how, with such a disposition and a great deal of common sense, he has committed the signal error of marrying, at the age of fifty-five, a young and pretty woman, and a creole, I believe, in the bargain.

"Monsieur de Breuilly!" said the marquis, as he presented me to the punctilious gentleman, "my best friend, who will infallibly become yours also, and who, quite as infallibly, will cut your throat if you attempt to show any attention to his wife."

"Mon Dieu! my dear friend," replied Monsieur de Breuilly, with a laugh that was anything but joyful, and accentuating each word in his peculiar style, "why represent me to this gentleman as a Norman Othello? Monsieur may surely—monsieur is perfectly free to—besides, he knows and can observe the proper limits of things. At any rate, sir, here is Madame de Breuilly; suffer me to recommend her myself to your kind attentions."

Somewhat surprised at this language, I had the simplicity, or perhaps the innocent malice, of interpreting it literally. I sat down squarely by the side of Madame de Breuilly, and I began paying her marked attention, while, however, "observing the proper limits of things." In the meantime, Monsieur de Breuilly was watching us from a distance, with an extraordinary countenance. I could see his little gray eyes sparkling like glowing ashes; he was laughing loud, grinning, stamping, and fairly disjointing his fingers with sinister cracks. Monsieur de Malouet came suddenly to me, handed me a whist card, and taking me aside:

"What the duse has got into you?" he said.

"Into me? why, nothing!"

"Have I not warned you? It's quite a serious matter. Look at Breuilly! It is the only weakness of that gallant man; every one respects it here. Do likewise, I beg of you."

From the weakness of that gallant man, it results that his wife is condemned in society to perpetual quarantine. The fighting propensities of a husband are often but an additional attraction for the lightning; but men hesitate to risk their lives without any prospect of possible compensation, and we have here a man who threatens you at least with a public scandal, not only before harvest, as they say, but even before the seed has been fairly sown. Such a state of affairs manifestly discourages the most enterprising, and it is quite rare that Madame de Breuilly has not two vacant seats on her right and on her left, despite her nonchalant grace, despite her great creole eyes, and despite her plaintive and beseeching looks, that seem to be ever saying: "Mon Dieu! will no one lead me into temptation?"

You would doubtless think that the evident neglect in which the poor wife lives ought to be, for her husband, a motive of security. Not at all! His ingenious mania manages to discover in that fact a fresh motive of perplexity.

"My friend," he was saying yesterday to Monsieur de Malouet, "you know that I am no more jealous than any one else; but without being Orosmane, I do not pretend to be George Dandin. Well! one thing troubles me, my friend; have you noticed that apparently no one pays any attention to my wife?"

"Parbleu! if that's what troubles you—"

"Of course it is; you must admit that it is not natural. My wife is pretty; why don't they pay attention to her as well as to other ladies? There is something suspicious there!"

Fortunately, and to the great advantage of the social question, all the young women who reside in turn at the chateau are not guarded by dragons of that caliber. A few even, and among them two or three Parisians out for a holiday, display a freedom of manner, a love of pleasure, and an exaggerated elegance that certainly pass the bounds of discretion. You are aware that I have not the highest opinion of that sort of behavior, which does not answer my idea of the duties of a woman, and even of a woman of the world; nevertheless, I take side without hesitation with these giddy ones; and their conduct even appears to me the very ideal of truth and sincerity, when I hear nightly certain pious matrons distilling against them, amid low and vulgar gossip, the venom of the basest envy that can swell a rural heart. Moreover, it is not always necessary to leave Paris in order to have the ugly spectacle of these provincials let loose against what they call vice, namely, youth, elegance, distinction, charm—in a word, all the qualities which the worthy ladies possess no more, or have perhaps never possessed.

Nevertheless, with whatever disgust, these chaste vixens inspire me for the virtue they pretend to uphold (Oh, virtue! how many crimes are committed in thy name!), I am compelled, to my great regret to agree with them on one point, and to admit that one of their victims at least gives an appearance of justice to their reprobation and to their calumnies. The angel of kindness himself would hide his face in presence of this complete specimen of dissipation, of turbulence, of futility, and finally of worldly extravagance that bears the name of Countess de Palme, and the nickname of the Little Countess; a rather ill-fitting nickname, by the way, for the lady is not small, but simply slender and lithe. Madame de Palme is twenty-five years of age; she is a widow; she spends the winter in Paris with her sister, and the summer in an old Norman manor-house, with her aunt, Madame de Pontbrian. Let me get rid of the aunt first.

This aunt, who is of very ancient nobility, is particularly noted for the fervor of her hereditary opinions, and for her strict devotion. Those are both claims to consideration which I admit fully, so far as I am concerned. Every solid principle and every sincere sentiment command in these days a peculiar respect. Unfortunately Madame de Pontbrian seems to be one of those intensely devout persons who are but very indifferent Christians. She is one of those who, reducing to a few minor observances, of which they are ridiculously proud, all the duties of their religious or political faith, impart to both a harsh and hateful appearance, the effect of which is not exactly to attract proselytes. The outer forms, in all things, are sufficient for her conscience; otherwise, no trace of charity or kindness; above all, no trace of humility. Her genealogy, her assiduity to church, and her annual pilgrimages to the shrine of an illustrious exile (who would probably be glad to dispense with the sight of her countenance), inspire in this fairy such a lofty idea of herself and such a profound contempt for her neighbor, that they make her positively unsociable. She remains forever absorbed in the latrian worship which she believes due to herself. She deigns to speak but to God, and He must indeed be a kind and merciful God if He listens to her.

Under the nominal patronage of this mystic duenna, the Little Countess enjoys an absolute independence, which she uses to excess. After spending the winter in Paris, where she kills off regularly two horses and a coachman every month for the sole gratification of waltzing ten minutes every night in half a dozen different balls, Madame de Palme feels the necessity of seeking rest in the peace of rural life. She arrives at her aunt's, she jumps upon a horse, and she starts at full gallop. It matters not which way she goes, provided she keeps going. Most generally she comes to the Chateau de Malouet, where the kind-hearted mistress of the house manifests for her an amount of predilection which I can hardly understand. Familiar with men, impertinent with women, the Little Countess offers a broad mark to the most indiscreet homage of the former, and to the jealous hostility of the latter. Indifferent to the outrages of public opinion, she seems ready to aspire to the coarsest incense of gallantry; but what she requires above all things is noise, movement, a whirl, worldly pleasure carried to its most extreme and most extravagant fury; what she requires every morning, every evening, and every night, is a breakneck chase, which she conducts with frenzy; a reckless game, in which she may break the bank; an uninterrupted German, which she leads until dawn. A stoppage of a single minute, a moment of rest, of meditation and reflection, would kill her. Never was an existence at once so busy and so idle; never a more unceasing and more sterile activity.

Thus she goes through life hurriedly and without a halt, graceful, careless, busy, and ignorant as the horse she rides. When she reaches the fatal goal, that woman will fall from the nothingness of her agitation into the nothingness of eternal rest, without the shadow of a serious idea, the faintest notion of duty, the lightest cloud of a thought worthy a human being, having ever grazed, even in a dream, the narrow brain that is sheltered behind her pure, smiling, and stupid brow. It might be said that death, at whatever age it may overtake her, will find the Little Countess just as she left the cradle, if it were possible to suppose that she has preserved its innocence as well as she has retained its profound puerility. Has that madcap a soul? The word nothingness has escaped me. It is indeed difficult for me to conceive what might survive that body when it has once lost the vain fever and the frivolous breath that seem alone to animate it.

I know too well the miserable ways of the world, to take to the letter the accusations of immorality of which Madame de Palme is here the object on the part of the witches, as also on the part of some of her rivals who are silly enough to envy her social success. It is not in that respect, as you may understand, that I treat her with so much severity. Men, when they show themselves unmerciful for certain errors, are too apt to forget that they have all, more or less, spent part of their lives seeking to bring them about for their own benefit. But there is in the feminine type which I have just sketched something more shocking than immorality itself, which, however, it is rather difficult to separate from it. And so, notwithstanding my desire of not making myself conspicuous in anything, I have been unable to take upon myself to join the throng of admirers whom Madame de Palme drags after her triumphal car. I know not whether

"Le tyran dans sa cour remarqua mon absence:"

I am sometimes tempted to believe it, from the glances of astonishment and scorn with which I am overwhelmed when we meet; but it is more simple to attribute these hostile symptoms to the natural antipathy that separates two creatures as dissimilar as we are. I look at her at times, myself, with the gaping surprise which must be excited in the mind of any thinking being by the monstrosity of such a psychological phenomenon. In that way we are even. I ought rather to say we were even, for we are really no longer so, since a rather cruel little adventure that happened to me last night, and which constitutes in my account-current with Madame de Palme a considerable advance, which she will find it difficult to make up. I have told you that Madame de Malouet, through I know not what refinement of Christian charity, manifested a genuine predilection for the Little Countess. I was talking with the marquise last evening in a corner of the drawing-room. I took the liberty of telling her that this predilection, coming from a woman like her, was a bad example; that I had never very well understood, for my part, that passage of the Holy Scriptures in which the return of a single sinner is celebrated above the constant merit of a thousand just, and that this had always appeared to me very discouraging for the just.

"In the first place," answered Madame de Malouet, "the just do not get discouraged; and in the next place, there are none. Do you fancy yourself one, by chance?"

"Certainly not; I am perfectly well aware of the contrary."

"Well, then, where do you get the right of judging your neighbor so severely?"

"I do not acknowledge Madame de Palme as my neighbor."

"That's convenient! Madame de Palme, sir, has been badly brought up, badly married, and always spoilt; but, believe me, she is a genuine rough diamond."

"I only see the roughness."

"And rest assured that it only requires a skillful workman—I mean a good husband—to cut and polish it."

"Allow me to pity that future lapidary."

Madame de Malouet tapped the carpet with her foot, and manifested other signs of impatience, which I knew not at first how to interpret, for she is never out of humor; but suddenly a thought, which I took for a luminous one, occurred in my mind; I had no doubt that I had at last discovered the weak side and the only failing in that charming old woman. She was possessed with the mania of match making, and, in her Christian anxiety to snatch the Little Countess from the abyss of perdition, she was secretly meditating to hurl me into it with her, unworthy though I be. Penetrated with this modest conviction, I kept upon a defensive that seems to me, at the present moment, perfectly ridiculous.

"Mon Dieu!" said Madame de Malouet, "because you doubt her learning!"

"I do not doubt her learning," I said; "I doubt whether she knows how to read."

"But, in short, what fault do you find with her?" rejoined Madame de Malouet in a singularly agitated tone of voice.

I determined to demolish, at a single stroke, the matrimonial dream with which I supposed the marchioness to be deluding herself.

"I find fault with her," I replied, "for giving to the world the spectacle, supremely irritating even for a profane being like me, of triumphant nullity and haughty vice. I am not worth much, it's true, and I have no right to judge, but there is in me, as well as in any theatrical audience, a certain sentiment of reason and morality that rises in indignation in presence of personages wholly devoid of common-sense or virtue, and that protests against their triumph."

The old lady's indignation seemed to increase.

"Do you think I would receive her, if she deserved all the stones which slander casts at her?"

"I think it is impossible for you to believe any evil."

"Bah! I assure you that you do not show in this case any evidence of penetration. These love stories which are attributed to her are so little like her! She is a child who does not even know what it is to love!"

"I am convinced of that, madame. Her commonplace coquetry is sufficient evidence of that. I am even ready to swear that the allurements of the imagination or the impulses of passion are wholly foreign to her errors, which thus remain without excuse."

"Oh! mon Dieu!" exclaimed Madame de Malouet, clasping her hands, "do hush! she is a poor, forsaken child! I know her better than you do. I assure you that beneath her appearance—much too frivolous, I admit—she possesses in fact as much heart as she does sense."

"That is precisely what I think, madam; as much one of as of the other."

"Ah! that is really intolerable," murmured Madame de Malouet, dropping her arms in a disconsolate manner.

At the same moment, I saw the curtain that half covered the door by the side of which we sat shake violently, and the Little Countess, leaving the hiding place where she had been confined by the exigencies of I know not what game, showed herself to us for a moment in the aperture of the door, and returned to join the group of players that stood in the adjoining parlor. I looked at Madame de Malouet:

"What! she was there!"

"Of course she was. She heard us, and, what's more, she could see us. I made all the signs I could, but you were off!"

I remained somewhat embarrassed. I regretted the harshness of my words; for, in attacking so violently this young person, I had yielded to the excitement of controversy much more than to a sentiment of serious animadversion. In point of fact, she is indifferent to me, but it's a little too much to hear her praised.

"And now what am I to do?" I said to Madame de Malouet.

She reflected for a moment, and replied with a slight shrug of her shoulders:

"*Ma foi!* nothing; that's the best thing you can do."

The least breath causes a full cup to overflow; thus the little unpleasantness of this scene seems to have intensified this feeling of ennui which has scarce left me since my advent into this abode of joy. This continuous gayety, this restless agitation, this racing and dancing and dining, this ceaseless merrymaking, and this eternal round of festivity importune me to the point of disgust. I regret bitterly the time I have wasted in reading and investigations which in no wise concern my official mission and have but little advanced its termination; I regret the engagements which the kind entreaties of my hosts have extorted from my weakness; I regret my vale of Tempe; above all, Paul, I regret you. There are certainly in this little social center a sufficient number of superior and kindly disposed minds to form the elements of the pleasantest and even the most elevated relations; but these elements are fairly submerged in the worldly and vulgar throng, and can only be eliminated from it with much trouble and difficulty, and never without admixture. Monsieur and Madame de Malouet, Monsieur de Breuilly even, when his insane jealously does not deprive him of the use of his faculties, certainly possess choice minds and hearts; but the mere difference of age opens an abyss between us. As to the young men and the men of my own age whom I meet here, they all march with more or less eager step in Madame de Palme's wake. It is enough that I should decline to follow them in that path, to cause them to manifest toward me a coolness akin to antipathy. My pride does not attempt to break that ice, though two or three among them appear well gifted, and reveal instincts superior to the life they have adopted.

There is one question I sometimes ask of myself on that subject; are we any better, you and I, youthful Paul, than this crowd of joyous companions and pleasant *viveurs*, or are we simply different from them? Like ourselves, they possess honesty and honor; like ourselves, they have neither virtue nor religion properly so-called. So far, we are equal. Our tastes alone and our pleasures differ; all their preoccupations turn to the lighter ways of the world, to the cares of gallantry and material activity; ours are almost exclusively given up to the exercise of thought, to the talents of the mind, to the works, good or evil, of the intellect. In the light of human truth, and according to common estimation, it is doubtful whether the difference in this particular is wholly in our favor; but in a more elevated order, in the moral order, and, so to speak, in the presence of God, does that superiority hold good? Are we merely yielding, as they do, to an inclination that leads us rather more to one side than to another, or are we obeying an imperative duty? What is in the eyes of God the merit of intellectual life? It seems to me sometimes that we possess for thought a species of pagan worship to which He attaches no value, and which perhaps even offends Him. More frequently, however, I think that He wishes us to make use of thought, were it even to be turned against Him, and that He accepts as a homage all the quiverings of that noble instrument of joy and torture which He has placed within us.

Is not sadness, in periods of doubt and anxiety, a species of religion? I trust so. We are, you and I, somewhat like those poor dreaming sphinxes who have been asking in vain for so many centuries, from the solitudes of the desert, the solution of the eternal riddle. Would it be a greater and more guilty folly than the happy carelessness of the Little Countess? We shall see. In the meantime, retain, for my sake, that ground-work of melancholy upon which you weave your own gentle mirth; for, thank God! you are not a pedant; you can live, you can laugh, and even laugh aloud; but thy soul is sad unto death, and that is only why I love unto death thy fraternal soul.

CHAPTER VI.

The Marquise Intercedes.

1st October.

Paul, there is something going on here that does not please me. I would like to have your advice; send it as soon as possible.

On Thursday morning, after finishing my letter, I went down to give it to the messenger, who leaves quite early; then, as it only wanted a few minutes of the breakfast-hour, I walked into the drawing-room, which was still empty. I was quietly looking over a review by the fireside, when the door was suddenly flung open; I heard the crushing and rustling of a silk dress too broad to get easily through an aperture three feet wide, and I saw the Little Countess appear: she had spent the night at the chateau.

If you remember the unfortunate conversation in which I had become entangled, the previous evening, and which Madame de Palme had overheard from beginning to end, you will readily understand that this lady was the last person in the world with whom it might prove pleasant to find myself alone that morning.

I rose and I addressed to her a deep courtsey; she replied with a nod, which, though slight, was still more than I deserved from her. The first steps she took in the parlor after she had seen me were stamped with hesitation and a sort of wavering; it was like the action of a partridge lightly hit on the wing and somewhat stunned by the shot. Would she go to the piano, to the window, to the right or to the left, or opposite? It was clear that she did not know herself; but indecision is not the weak point of her disposition; she soon made up her mind, and crossing the immense drawing room with very firm step, she came in the direction of the chimney, that is, toward my immediate domain.

Standing in front of my armchair with my review in my hand, I was awaiting the event with an apparent gravity that concealed but imperfectly, I fear, a rather powerful inward anxiety. I had indeed every reason to apprehend an explanation and a scene. In every circumstance of this kind, the natural feelings of our heart and the refinement which education and the habits of society add to them, the absolute freedom of the attack and the narrow limits allowed to the defense, give to women an overwhelming superiority over any man who is not a boor or a lover. In the particular crisis that was threatening me, the stinging consciousness of my wrongs, the recollection of the almost insulting form under which my offense had manifested itself, united to deprive me of all thought of resistance; I found myself delivered over, bound hand and foot, to the frightful wrath of a young and imperious woman thirsting for vengeance. My attitude was, therefore, not very brilliant.

Madame de Palme stopped within two steps of me, spread her right hand on the marble of the mantel, and extended toward the blazing hearth the bronzed slipper within which her left foot was held captive. Having accomplished these preliminary dispositions, she turned toward me, and without addressing me a single word, she seemed to enjoy my countenance, which, I repeat, was not worth much. I resolved to sit down again and resume my reading; but previously, and by way of transition, I thought best to say politely:

"Wouldn't you like to have this review, madam?"

"Thank you, sir, I cannot read."

Such was the answer that was promptly shot off at me in a brief tone of voice. I made with my head and my hand a courteous gesture, by which I seemed to sympathize gently with the infirmity that was thus revealed to me, after which I sat down, feeling more easy. I had drawn my adversary's fire. Honor seemed to me satisfied.

Nevertheless, after a few moments of silence, I began again to feel the awkwardness of my situation; I strove in vain to become absorbed in my reading; I kept seeing a multitude of little bronzed slippers dancing all over the paper. An open scene would have appeared to me decidedly preferable to this unpleasant and persistent proximity, to the mute hostility betrayed to my furtive glance by Madame de Palme's restless foot, the jingle of her rings on the marble mantel, and the quivering mobility of her nostrils. I therefore unconsciously uttered a sigh of relief when the door, opening suddenly, introduced upon the stage a new personage, whom I felt justified in considering as an ally.

It was a lady—a school friend of Lady A——, whose name is

Madame Durmaitre. She is a widow, and extremely handsome; she is noted for a lesser degree of folly amid the wild and worldly ladies of the chateau. For this reason, and somewhat also on account of her superior charms, she has long since conquered the ill-will of Madame de Palme, who, in allusion to her rival's somber style of dress, to the languid character of her beauty, and to the somewhat elegiac turn of her conversation, is pleased to designate her, among the young people, as the Malabar Widow. Madame Durmaitre is positively lacking in wit; but she is intelligent, tolerably well read, and much inclined to reverie. She prides herself upon a certain talent for conversation. Seeing that I am myself destitute of any other social accomplishment, she has got it into her head that I must possess that particular one, and she has undertaken to make sure of it. The result has been, between us, a rather assiduous and almost cordial intercourse; for, if I have been unable to fully respond to all her hopes, I listen, at least with religious attention, to the little melancholy pathos which is habitual with her. I appear to understand her, and she seems grateful for it. The truth is that I never tire hearing her voice, which is musical, gazing at her features, which are exquisitely regular, and admiring her large black eyes, over which a fringe of heavy eyelashes casts a mystic shadow. However, do not feel uneasy; I have decided that the time for being loved, and consequently for loving, is over for me; now, love is a malady which no one need fear, if he sincerely strive to repress its first symptoms.

Madame de Palme had turned around at the sound of the opening door; when she recognized Madame Durmaitre, a fierce light gleamed in her blue eyes; chance had sent her a victim. She allowed the beautiful widow to advance a few paces toward us, with the slow and mournful step which is characteristic of her manner, and bursting out laughing:

"Bravo!" she exclaimed, with emphasis, "the march to the scaffold! the victim dragged to the altar! Iphigenia; or, rather, Hermione:

"'Pleurante apres son char vous voulez qu'on me voie!'

"Who is it that has written this verse? I am so ignorant! Ah! it's your friend, M. de Lamartine, I believe. He was thinking of you, my dear!"

"Ah! you quote poetry now, dear madam," said Madame

Durmaitre, who is not very skilled at retort.

"Why not, dear madam? Have you a monopoly of it?—'Pleurante apres son char?' I have heard Rachel say that. By the way, it is not by Lamartine, it's by Boileau. I must tell you, dear Nathalie, that I intend to ask you to give me lessons in serious and virtuous conversation. It's so amusing! And to begin at once, come! tell me whom you prefer, Lamartine or Boileau?"

"But, Bathilde, there is no connection," replied Madame Durmaitre, rather sensibly and much too candidly.

"Ah!" rejoined Madame de Palme. And suddenly pointing me out with her finger: "You perhaps prefer this gentleman, who also writes poetry?"

"No, madam," I said, "it is a mistake; I write none."

"Ah! I thought you did. I beg your pardon."

Madame Durmaitre, who doubtless owes the unalterable serenity of her soul to the consciousness of her supreme beauty, had been content with smiling with disdainful nonchalance. She dropped into the armchair, which I had given up to her.

"What gloomy weather!" she said to me; "really, this autumnal sky weighs upon the soul. I was looking out of the window; all the trees look like cypress-trees, and the whole country looks like a graveyard. It would really seem that—"

"No, ah! no. I beg of you, Nathalie," interrupted Madame de Palme, "say no more. That's enough fun before breakfast. You'll make yourself sick."

"Well, now! my dear Bathilde, you must really have slept very badly last night," said the beautiful widow.

"I, my dear? ah! do not say that. I had celestial, ecstatic dreams; ecstasies, you know. My soul held converse with other souls—like your own soul. Angels smiled at me through the foliage of the cypress-trees—and so forth, and so forth!"

Madame Durmaitre blushed slightly, shrugged her shoulders, and took up the review I had laid upon the mantelpiece.

"By the bye, Nathalie," resumed Madame de Palme, "do you know who we are going to have at dinner today, in the way of men?" The good-natured Nathalie mentioned Monsieur de Breuilly, two or three other married gentlemen, and the parish priest.

"Then I am going away after breakfast," said the Little Countess, looking at me.

"That's very polite to us," murmured Madame Durmaitre.

"You know," replied the other with imperturbable assurance, "that I only like men's society, and there are three classes of individuals whom I do not consider as belonging to that sex, or to any other; those are married men, priests, and savants."

As she concluded this sentence, Madame de Palme cast another glance at me, by which however, I had no need to understand that she included me in her classification of neutral species; it could only be among the individuals of the third category, though I have no claim to it whatever; but it does not require much to be considered a savant by the ladies.

Almost at this very moment, the breakfast bell rang in the courtyard of the chateau, and she added:

"Ah! there's breakfast, thank Heaven! for I am develish hungry, with all respect for pure spirits and troubled souls."

She then ran and skipped to the other end of the parlor to greet Monsieur de Malouet, who was coming in followed by his guests. As to myself, I promptly offered my arm to Madame Durmaitre, and I endeavored by earnest attentions, to make her forget the storm which the mere shade of sympathy she manifests toward me had just attracted upon her.

As you may have remarked, the Little Countess had exhibited in the course of this scene, as always, an unmeasured and unseemly freedom of language; but she displayed greater resources of mind than I supposed her capable of doing, and though they had been directed against me, I could not help feeling thankful to her—to such an extent do I hate fools, whom I have ever found in this world more pernicious than wicked people. The result was, that with the feeling of repulsion and contempt with which the extravagantly worldly woman inspired me, there was henceforth mingled a shade of gentle pity for the badly brought-up child and the misdirected woman.

Women are prompt in catching delicate shades of feeling, and the latter did not escape Madame de Palme. She became vaguely conscious of a slightly favorable change in my opinion of her, and it was not long before she even began to exaggerate its extent and to attempt abusing it. For two days she pursued me with her keenest shafts, which I bore good-naturedly, and to which I even responded with some little attentions, for I had still at heart the rude expressions of my dialogue with Madame de Malouet, and I did not think I had sufficiently expiated them by the feeble martyrdom I had undergone the following day in common with the beautiful Malabar Widow.

This was enough to cause Madame Bathilde de Palme to imagine that she could treat me as a conquered province, and add Ulysses to his companions. Day before yesterday she had tested several times during the day the extent of her growing power over my heart and my will, by asking two or three little services of me; services to the honor of which every one here eagerly aspires, and which for my part, I discharged politely but with evident coolness.

In spite of the extreme reserve with which I had lent myself to these trials during the day, Madame de Palme believed in her complete success; she hastily judged that she now had but to rivet my chains and bind me to her triumph, a feeble addition of glory assuredly, but which had, after all, the merit, in her eyes, of having been contested. During the evening, as I was leaving the whist-table, she advanced toward me deliberately, and requested me to do her the honor of figuring with her in the character dance called the cotillon.[2] I excused myself laughingly on my complete inexperience; she insisted, declaring that I had evident dispositions for dancing, and reminding me of the agility I had displayed in the forest. Finally, and to close the debate, she led me away familiarly by the arm, adding that she was not in the habit of being refused.

"Nor I, madam," I said, "in that of making a show of myself."

"What! not even to gratify me?"

"Not even for that, madam, and were it the only means of succeeding in doing so."

I bowed to her smilingly after these words, which I had emphasized in such a positive manner that she insisted no more. She

2   The German.

dropped my arm abruptly and returned to join a group of dancers who were observing us at a distance with manifest interest. She was received by them with whispers and smiles, to which she replied with a few rapid sentences, among which I only caught the word *revanche*. I paid no further attention to the matter for the time being, and my soul went to converse amid the clouds with the soul of Madame Durmaitre.

The next day a grand hunt was to take place in the forest. I had arranged to take no share in it, wishing to make the best of a whole day of solitude to push forward my hopeless undertaking. Toward noon, the hunters met in the courtyard of the chateau, which rang again for some fifteen minutes with the loud blast of the trumpets, the stamping of horses, and the yelping of the pack. Then the tumultuous crowd disappeared down the avenue, the noise gradually died away, and I remained master of myself and of my mind, in the midst of a silence the more grateful that it is the more rare on this meridian.

I had been enjoying my solitude for a few minutes, and I was turning over the folio pages of the *Neustra pia*, while smiling at my own happiness, when I fancied I heard the gallop of a horse in the avenue, and soon after on the pavement of the court. Some hunter behind time, I thought, and, taking up my pen, I began extracting from the enormous volume the passage relating to the General Chapters of the Benedictines; but a new and more serious interruption came to afflict me; some one was knocking at the library door. I shook my head with ill-humor, and I said "Come in!" in the same tone in which I might have said "Go away!" Some one did come in. I had seen, a few moments before, Madame de Palme taking her flight, feathers and all, at the head of the cavalcade, and I was not a little surprised to find her again within two steps of me as soon as the door was open. Her head was bare, and her hair was tucked up behind in an odd manner; she held her whip in one hand, and with the other lifted up the long train of her riding-habit. The excitement of the rapid ride she had just had seemed further to intensify the expression of audacity which is habitual to her look and to her features. And yet her voice was less assured than usual when she exclaimed as she came in:

"Ah! I beg your pardon! I thought Madame de Malouet was here?"

I had risen at once to my full height.

"No, madam, she is not here."

"Ah! excuse me. Do you know where she is?"

"I do not, madam; but I can go and ascertain, if you wish."

"Thanks, thanks! I'll find her easily enough. The fact is, I met with a little accident."

"Indeed!"

"Oh, not much! a trailing limb tore the band off my hat, and my feathers dropped off."

"Your blue feathers, madam?"

"Yes, my blue feathers. In short, I have returned to the chateau to have my hat-band sewed on again. You are comfortable there to work?"

"Perfectly so, madam, I could not be better."

"Are you very busy just now?"

"Well, yes, madam, rather busy."

"Ah! I am sorry."

"Why so?"

"Because, I had an idea. I thought of asking you to accompany me to the forest. The gentlemen will be nearly there when I am ready to start again—and I cannot very well go on alone so far."

While lisping this somewhat confused explanation, the Little Countess had an expression at once sly and embarrassed, which greatly fortified the sentiment of distrust which the awkwardness of her entrance had excited in my mind.

"Madam," I said, "you really distress me. I shall regret all my life to have missed the delightful occasion you are kind enough to offer me; but it is indispensable that tomorrow's mail shall carry off this report, which the minister is expecting with extreme impatience."

"You are afraid to lose your situation?"

"I have none to lose, madam."

"Well, then, let the minister wait, for my sake; it will flatter me."

"That is impossible, madam."

She assumed a very dry tone:

"But, that is really strange! What! you are not more anxious to be agreeable to me?"

"Madam," I replied rather dryly in my turn, "I should be extremely anxious to be agreeable to you, but I am not at all anxious to help you win your wager."

I threw out that insinuation somewhat at random, resting it upon some recollections and some slight indications which you may have been able to collect here and there in the course of my narrative. Nevertheless, I had hit it exactly. Madame de Palme blushed up to her ear, stammered out two or three words which I failed to catch, and left the room, having lost all countenance.

This precipitate retreat left me quite confused myself. I cannot admit that we should carry out our respect for the weaker sex so far as to lend ourselves to every caprice and every enterprise it may please a woman to direct against our peace or our dignity; but our right of legitimate self-defense in such encounters is circumscribed within narrow and delicate limits, which I feared I had overstepped. It was enough that Madame de Palme should be alone in the world, and without any other protection than her sex, to make it seem extremely painful to me to have thoughtlessly yielded to the irritation, just though it might be, which her impertinent insistence had aroused. As I was endeavoring to establish between our respective wrongs a balance that might serve to quiet my scruples, there was another knock at the library door. This time, it was Madame de Malouet who came in. She was much moved.

"Do tell me what has taken place," she said.

I gave her full and minute particulars of my interview with Madame de Palme, and, while expressing much regret at my vivacity, I added that the lady's conduct toward me was inexplicable; that she had taken me twice within twenty-four hours for the subject of her wagers, and that it was a great deal too much attention, on her part, for a man who asked her, as a sole favor, not to trouble herself about him any more than he troubled himself about her.

"Mon Dieu!" said the kind marquise, "I have no fault to find with you. I have been able to appreciate with my own eyes, during the past few days, your conduct and her own. But all this is very disagreeable. That child has just thrown herself in my arms weeping terribly. She says you have treated her like a creature—"

I protested: "I have repeated to you, word for word, madam, what passed between us."

"It was not your words, it was your expression, your tone. Monsieur George, let me speak frankly with you: are you afraid of falling in love with Madame de Palme?"

"Not in the least, madam."

"Are you anxious that she should fall in love with you?"

"Neither, I assure you."

"Well, then, do me a favor; lay aside your pride for one day, and escort Madame de Palme to the hunt."

"Madam!"

"The advice may seem singular to you. But rest assured that I do not offer it without mature reflection. The repulsion which you manifest for Madame de Palme is precisely what attracts toward you that imperious and spoilt child. She becomes irritated and obstinate in presence of a resistance to which she has not been accustomed. Be meek enough to yield to her fancy. Do that for me."

"Seriously madam, you think?—"

"I think," interrupted the old lady laughingly, "with due respect to you, that you will lose your principal merit in her eyes as soon as she sees you submit to her yoke like all the rest."

"Really, madam, you present things to me under an entirely novel aspect. It never occurred to me to attribute Madame de Palme's mischievous pranks to a sentiment of which I might have reason to be proud."

"And you have been quite right," she resumed sharply; "there is, thank heaven! nothing of the kind as yet; but it might have come and you are too fair a man to desire it, with the views which I know you to entertain."

"I trust myself wholly to your direction, madam; I am going too fetch my hat and gloves. The question is now, how Madame de Palme will receive my somewhat tardy civility."

"She will receive it very well, if you offer it with good grace."

"As to that, madam, I shall offer it with all the good grace I can command."

On this assurance, Madame de Malouet held out her hand, which I kissed with profound respect but rather slim gratitude.

When I entered the parlor, booted and spurred, Madame de Palme was alone there; deeply seated in an armchair, buried under her skirts, she was putting the finishing touches to her hat. She raised and dropped rapidly again her eyes, which were fiery red.

"Madam," I said, "I am sincerely so sorry to have offended you, that I venture to ask your pardon for an unpardonable piece of rudeness. I have come to hold myself at your disposition; if you decline my escort, you will not only be inflicting upon me an amply deserved mortification, but you will leave me still more unhappy than I have been guilty, and that is saying a great deal." Madame de Palme, taking into consideration the emotion of my voice rather more than my diplomatic pathos, lifted her eyes upon me again, opened her lips slightly, said nothing, and finally advanced a somewhat tremulous hand, which I hastened to receive within my own. She availed herself at once of this *point d'appui* to get on her feet, and bounded lightly to the floor. A few minutes later, we were both on horseback and leaving the courtyard of the chateau.

We reached the extremity of the avenue without having exchanged a single word. I felt deeply, as you may believe, how much this silence, on my part at least, was awkward, stiff, and ridiculous; but, as it often happens in circumstances which demand most imperatively the resources of eloquence, I was stricken with an invincible sterility of mind. I tried in vain to find some plausible subject of conversation, and the more annoyed I felt at finding none, the less capable I became of doing so.

"Suppose we have a run?" said Madame de Palme suddenly.

"Let us have a run!" I said; and we started at a gallop, to my infinite relief.

Nevertheless, it became absolutely necessary to check our speed at the entrance of the tortuous path that leads down into the valley of the ruins. The care required to guide our horses during that difficult descent served for a few minutes longer as a pretext for my silence; but, on reaching the level ground of the valley, I saw that I must speak at any cost, and I was about to begin with some commonplace remark, when Madame de Palme was kind enough to anticipate me:

"They say, sir, that you are very witty?"

"You may judge for yourself, madam," I replied laughingly.

"Rather difficult so far, even if I were able, which you are very far from conceding. Oh! you need not deny it! Its perfectly useless, after the conversation which chance made me overhear the other night."

"I have made so many mistakes concerning you, madam, you must realize the pitiful confusion I feel toward you."

"And in what respect have you been mistaken?"

"In all respects, I believe."

"You are not quite sure? Admit at least that I am a good-natured woman."

"Oh! with all my heart, madam!"

"You said that well. I believe you think it. You are not bad either, I believe, and yet you have been cruelly so to me."

"That is true."

"What sort of man are you, then, pray?" resumed the Little Countess in her brief and abrupt tone; "I cannot understand it very well. By what right, on what ground, do you despise me? Suppose I am really guilty of all the intrigues which are attributed to me; what is that to you? Are you a saint yourself? a reformer? Have you never gone astray? Are you any more virtuous than other men of your age and condition? What right have you to despise me? Explain!"

"Were I guilty of the sentiments which you attribute to me, madam, I should answer, that never has any one, either in your sex or mine, taken his own morality as the rule of his opinion and his judgment upon others; we live as we can, and we judge as we should; it is more particularly a very frequent inconsistency among men, to frown down unmercifully the very weaknesses which they encourage and of which they derive the benefit. For my part, I hold severely aloof from a degree of austerity as ridiculous in a man as unchari-table in a Christian. And as to that unfortunate conversation which a deplorable chance caused you to hear, and in which my expressions, as it always happens, went far beyond the measure of my thought, it is an offense which I can never obliterate, I know; but I shall at least explain frankly. Every one has his own tastes and his own way of understanding life in this world; we differ so much, you and I, and you conceived for me, at first sight, an extreme antipathy. This dispo-sition, which, on one side at least, madam, was to be singularly modi-fied on better acquaintance, prompted me to some thoughtless manifestations of ill-humor and vivacity of controversy. You have doubtless suffered, madam, from the violence of my language, but much less, I beg you to believe, than I was to suffer from it myself, after I had recognized its profound and irreparable injustice."

This apology, more sincere than lucid, drew forth no answer. We were at this moment just coming out of the old abbey church, and we found ourselves unexpectedly mingled in the last ranks of the caval-cade. Our appearance caused a suppressed murmur to run through the dense crowd of hunters. Madame de Palme was at once sur-rounded by a merry throng that seemed to address congratulations to her on the winning of her wager. She received them with an indif-ferent and pouting look, whipped up her horse, and made her way to the front before entering the forest.

In the meantime, Monsieur de Malouet had received me with still more cordial affability than usual, and without making any direct allusion to the accident which had brought me against my will to this cynegetic feast, he omitted no attention that could make me forget its trifling annoyance. Soon after the hounds started a deer, and I followed them with keen relish, being by no means indifferent to that manly pastime, though it is not sufficient for my happiness in this world.

The pack was thrown off the scent two or three times, and the deer had the best of the day. At about four o'clock we started on our way back to the chateau. When we crossed the valley on our return, the twilight was already marking out more clearly upon the sky the outline of the trees and the crest of the hills; a melancholy shade was falling upon the woods, and a whitish fog chilled the grass on the meadows, while a thicker mist indicated the sinuous course of the little river. As I remained absorbed in the contemplation of the scene which reminded me of better days, I discovered suddenly Madame de Palme at my side.

"I believe, after due reflection," she said with her usual brusque-ness, "that you scorn my ignorance and my lack of wit much more than my supposed want of morality. You think less of virtue than you do of intelligence. Is that it?"

"Certainly not," I said, laughingly; "that isn't it; that isn't it at all. In the first place, the word scorn must be suppressed, having nothing to do here; then, I don't much believe in your ignorance, and not at all in your lack of wit. Finally, I see nothing above virtue, when I see it at all, which is not often. Furthermore, madam, I feel confused at the importance you attach to my opinion. The secret of my likes and dislikes is quite simple; I have, as I was telling you, the most religious respect for virtue, but all mine is limited to a deep-seated sentiment of a few essential duties which I practice as best I can; I could not therefore ask any more of others. As to the intellect, I confess that I value it greatly, and life seems too serious a matter to me to be treated on the footing of a perpetual ball, from the cradle to the grave. Moreover, the productions of the mind, works of art in particular, are the object of my most passionate preoccupations, and it is natural that I should like being able to speak of what interests me. That's all."

"Is it absolutely necessary to be forever talking of the ecstasies of the soul, of cemeteries, and the Venus of Milo, in order to obtain in your opinion the rank of a serious woman and a woman of taste? But, after all, you are right; I never think; if I did for one single minute, it seems to me that I should go mad, that my head would split. And what were you thinking about yourself, in that old convent cell?"

"I thought a great deal about you," I replied gayly, "on the evening of that day when you hunted me down so unmercifully, and I abused you most heartily."

"I can understand that." She began laughing, looking all around her, and added: "What a lovely valley! what a delightful evening! And now, are you still disposed to abuse me?"

"Now, I wish from the bottom of my soul I were able to do something for your happiness."

"And I for yours," she said, quietly.

I bowed for all answer, and a brief pause followed:

"If I were a man," suddenly said Madame de Palme, "I believe I would like to be a hermit."

"Oh! what a pity!"

"That idea does not surprise you?"

"No, madam."

"Nothing from me would surprise you, I suppose. You believe

me capable of anything—of anything, perhaps even of being fond of you?"

"Why not? Greater wonders have been seen! Am I not fond of you myself at the present moment? That's a fine example to follow!"

"You must give me time to think about it?"

"Not long!"

"As long as it may be necessary. We are friends in the meantime?"

"If we are friends, there is nothing further to expect," I said, holding out my hand frankly to the Little Countess. I felt that she was pressing it lightly, and the conversation ended there. We had reached the top of the hills; it was now quite dark, and we galloped all the rest of the way to the chateau.

As I was coming down from my room for dinner, I met Madame de Malouet in the vestibule.

"Well!" she said, laughingly, "did you conform to the prescription?"

"Rigidly, madam."

"You showed yourself subjugated?

"I did, madam."

"Excellent! She is satisfied now, and so are you."

"Amen!" I said.

The evening passed off without further incident.

I took pleasure in doing for Madame de Palme some trifling services which she was no longer asking. She left the dance two or three times to come and address me some good-natured jests that passed through her brain, and when I withdrew, she followed me to the door with a smiling and cordial look.

I ask you now, friend Paul, to sift the precise meaning and the moral of this tale. You may perhaps judge, and I hope you will, that a chimerical imagination can alone magnify into an event this vulgar episode of society life; but if you see in the facts I have just told you the least germ of danger, the slightest element of a serious complication, tell me so; I'll break the engagements that were to detain me here some ten or twelve days longer, and I'll leave at once.

I do not love Madame de Palme; I cannot and will not love her. My opinion of her has evidently changed greatly; I look upon her henceforth as a good little woman. Her head is light and will always be so; her behavior is better than she gets credit for, though perhaps not as good as she represents it herself; finally, her heart has both weight and value. I feel some friendship for her, an affection that has something fraternal in it; but between her and me, nothing further is at all likely; the expanse of the heavens divides us. The idea of being her husband makes me burst out laughing, and though a sentiment which you will readily appreciate, the thought of being her lover inspires me with horror. As to her, I believe she may feel the shadow of a caprice, but not even the dawn of a passion. Here I am now upon her etagere with the rest of the figureheads, and I think, as does Madame de Malouet, that may be enough to satisfy her. However, what do you think of it yourself?

CHAPTER VII.

A Misdirected Passion.

7th October.

Dear Paul, I take part in your grief from the bottom of my heart. Allow me, however, to assure you, from the very details of your own letter that your dear mother's illness offers no alarming symptoms whatever. It is one of those painful but harmless crises which the approach of winter brings back upon her almost invariably every year, as you know. Patience therefore, and courage, I beseech you.

It requires, my friend, the formal expression of your wishes to induce me to venture upon mingling my petty troubles with your grave solicitude. As you anticipated in your wisdom and in your kind friendship, it was consolation and not advice that I stood in need of when I received your letter. My heart is not at peace, and, what is worse for me, neither is my conscience; and yet, I think I have done my duty. Have I understood it right or not? Judge for yourself.

I take up my situation toward Madame de Palme where I had left it in my last letter. The day after our mutual explanation, I took every care to maintain our relations upon the footing of good-fellowship on which they seemed established, and which constituted, in my idea, the only sort of intelligence desirable and even possible between us. It seemed to me, on that day, that she manifested the same vivacity and the same spirit as usual; yet I fancied that her voice and her look, when she addressed me, assumed a meek gravity which is not part of her usual disposition; but on the following days, though I had not deviated from the line of conduct I had marked out for myself, it became impossible for me not to notice that Madame de Palme had lost something of her gayety, and that a vague preoccupation clouded the serenity of her brow. I could see her dancing-partners surprised at her frequent absence of mind; she still followed the whirl, but she no longer led it. Under pretext of fatigue, she would leave suddenly and abruptly her partner's arm, in the midst of a waltz, to go and sit in some corner with a pensive and even a pouting look. If there happened to be a vacant seat next to mine, she threw herself into it, and began from behind her fan some whimsical and disjointed conversation like the following:

"If I cannot be a hermit, I am going to become a nun. What would you say, if you saw me enter a convent tomorrow?"

"I should say that you would leave it the day after tomorrow."

"You have no confidence in my resolutions?"

"When they are unwise, no."

"I can only form unwise ones, according to you?"

"According to me, you waltz admirably. When a person waltzes as you do, it's an art, almost a virtue."

"Is it customary to flatter one's friends?"

"I am not flattering you. I never speak a single word to you that I have not carefully weighed, and that is not the most earnest expression of my thought. I am a serious man, madam."

"It does not seem so when you are with me. I verily believe, however, you have undertaken to make me hate laughter as much as I used to like it."

"I do not understand you."

"How do you think I look tonight?"

"Dazzling!"

"That's too much! I know that I am not handsome."

"I don't say you are handsome, but you are extremely graceful."

"That's better; and it must be true, for I feel it. The Malabar Widow is really handsome."

"Yes, I should like to see her at the funeral pile."

"To jump into it with her?"

"Exactly."

"Do you expect to leave soon?"

"Next week, I believe."

"Will you come and see me in Paris?"

"If you will allow me."

"No, I don't allow you."

"And why not? great heavens!"

"In the first place, I don't think I am going back to Paris myself."

"That's a good reason. And where do you expect to go, madam?"

"I don't know. Let us make a pedestrian tour somewhere, you and I together; will you?"

"I should like nothing better. When shall we start?"

Et cetera. I shall not tire you, my friend, with the particulars of some dozen similar conversations, every occasion of which for four days Madame de Palme evidently sought. There was on her part a constantly growing effort to leave aside all commonplace topics, and impart to our interviews a character of greater intimacy; there was on mine an equal amount of obstinacy in confining them within the strictest limits of social jargon, and remaining resolutely on the ground of worldly futility.

I now come to the scene that was to bring this painful struggle to a close, and unfortunately prove all its vanity to me.

Monsieur and Madame de Malouet were giving last night a grand farewell ball to their daughter, whose husband has been recalled to his post of duty, and the whole neighborhood within a circuit of ten leagues had been summoned to the feast. Toward ten o'clock an immense crowd was overflowing the vast ground floor of the chateau, in which the elegant dresses, the lights, and the flowers were mingled in dazzling confusion. As I was trying to make my way into the main drawing-room, I found myself face to face with Madame de Malouet, who drew me slightly aside.

"Well! my dear sir," she said, "I do not like the looks of things."

"Mon Dieu! what is there new?"

"I don't know exactly, but be on your guard. Ah! mon Dieu! I have remarkable confidence in you, sir; you will not take advantage of her, will you?"

Her voice was tender and her eyes moist.

"You may rely upon me, madam; but I sincerely wish I had gone a week ago."

"Eh! mon Dieu! who could have foreseen such a thing? Hush! there she comes!"

I turned round and saw Madame de Palme coming out of the parlor; before her the throng opened with that timorous eagerness and that species of terror which the supreme elegance of one of society's queens generally inspires in our sex. For the first time, Madame de Palme appeared handsome to me; the expression of her countenance was wholly novel to me, and a weird animation gleamed in her eyes and transfigured her features.

"Am I to your taste?" she said.

I manifested by I know not what movement an assent, which was moreover but too evident to the keen eye of a woman.

"I was looking for you," she added, "to show you the conservatory; it's fairylike. Come!"

She took my arm, and we started in the direction of the conservatory door which opened at the other end of the parlor, extending as far as the park, through the vines and the perfumes of hundreds of exotic plants, all the splendors of the feast. While we were admiring the effect of the girandoles that sparkled amid the luxuriant tropical flora like the bright constellations of another hemisphere, several gentlemen came to claim Madame de Palme's hand for a waltz; she refused them all, though I was sufficiently disinterested to join my entreaties to theirs.

"Our respective roles seem to me somewhat inverted," she said: "it is I who am detaining you, and you wish to get rid of me!"

"Heaven preserve me from such an idea! but I am afraid lest you may deprive yourself, out of kindness to me, of a pleasure you are so fond of."

"No! I know very well that I seek you and you avoid me. It is rather absurd in the eyes of the world, but I care nothing for that. For this one evening at least, I mean to amuse myself as I like. I forbid you to disturb my happiness. I am really very happy. I have everything I require—beautiful flowers, excellent music around me, and a friend at my side. Only—and that's a dark spot on my blue sky—I am much more certain of the music and the flowers than I am of the friend."

"You are entirely wrong."

"Explain your conduct, then, once for all. Why will you never talk seriously with me? Why do you obstinately refuse to tell me one single word that savors of confidence, of intimacy—of friendship, in a word?"

"Please reflect for a minute, madam; where would that lead us to?"

"What is that to you? That would lead us where it would. It is singular that you should be more anxious about it than I am."

"Come, what would you think of me if I ventured to speak of

love to you?"

"I don't ask you to make love to me!" she said, sharply.

"I know it, madam; and yet it is the inevitable turn my language would take if it ceased for a moment to be frivolous and commonplace. Now, admit that there is one man in the world who could not speak of love to you without incurring your contempt, and that I am that very man. I cannot say that I am very much pleased with having placed myself in such a position; but, after all, it is so, and I cannot forget it."

"That is showing a great deal of judgment."

"That is showing a great deal of courage."

She shook her head with an air of doubt, and resumed after a moment of silence:

"Do you know that you have just spoken to me as if I were what is called a 'fast' woman?"

"Oh! madam!"

"Of course, you think that I can never attribute to a man who pays his addresses to me any but improper intentions. If it were so, I would deserve being called a 'fast' woman, and I do not. I know you don't believe it, but it is the pure truth, as there is a God—yes, as there is a God! God knows me, and I pray to Him much oftener than is thought. He has kept me from doing harm thus far, and I hope He will keep me from it forever; but it is a thing of which He has not the sole control—" She stopped for a moment, and then added in a firm tone:

"You can do much toward it."

"I, madam?"

"I have allowed you to take, I know not how—I really do not know how!—a great influence over my destiny. Will you be willing to use it? That is the question."

"And in what capacity could I do so, pray, madam?" I said slowly and in a tone of cold reserve.

"Ah!" she exclaimed, in a hoarse and energetic accent, "how can you ask me that? It is too hard! you humiliate me too much!"

She left my arm and returned abruptly into the parlor. I remained for some time uncertain as to what course to pursue. I thought first of following Madame de Palme and explaining to her that she was mistaken—which was true—as to the interrogative answer which had offended her. She had applied that answer to some thought that pervaded her mind, which I did not understand, or at least which her words had revealed to me much less clearly than she had imagined; but after thinking over it, I shrank from the new and formidable explanation which such a course must inevitably bring about.

I left the conservatory, and walked into the garden to escape the hum of the ballroom, which importuned my ears. The night was cold but beautiful. With my heart still filled with the bitterness of this scene, I wandered instinctively beyond the luminous zone projected around the chateau through the apertures of the resplendent windows. I walked rapidly toward a double row of spruce trees, crossed by a rustic bridge thrown over a small brook which divided the garden from the park, and where the shade was more dense. I had just reached this somber spot, when a hand was laid on my arm and stopped me; at the same time a short and troubled voice, which I could not mistake, said:

"I must speak to you!"

"Madam! for mercy's sake! in the name of Heaven! what are you doing? you will ruin your reputation! Do return to the house! Come, come, let me escort you back!"

I attempted to seize her arm, but she eluded my grasp.

"I want to speak to you—I have decided to do so. Oh, mon Dieu! how awkwardly I do go about it, don't I? You must believe me more than ever a miserable creature! and yet there is nothing in it, not a thing; it's the truth, the pure truth, mon ami! You are the first man for whose sake I have forgotten—all that I am now forgetting! Yes, the first! Never has any other man heard from my lips a single word of tenderness, never! And you do not believe!"

I took both her hands in mine:

"I believe you, I swear it—I swear that I esteem you—that I respect you as a beloved daughter—but listen to me; pray, listen! do not brave openly this pitiless world—return to the ballroom—I'll join you there soon, I promise you—but in the name of Heaven, do not compromise your fair fame!"

The poor child melted into tears, and I felt that she was staggering; I supported her and helped her to a seat on a bench close by. I remained standing before her, holding one of her hands. The darkness was intense around us; I gazed into space, and I listened, in a state of vague stupor, to the clear and regular murmur of the brook flowing under the spruce trees, to the convulsive sobs that swelled the unhappy woman's bosom, and to the odious sounds of revelry which the orchestra sent us at intervals from afar. It was one of those moments that can never be forgotten.

She succeeded in mastering her grief at last, and seemed, after this explosion, to recover all her firmness.

"Monsieur," she said, rising and withdrawing her hand, "have no fears about my reputation. The world is accustomed to my follies. However, I have taken care that the present one shall not be noticed. Besides, I would not care if it was. You are the only man whose esteem I have ever desired, and, unfortunately the only one also whose contempt I have incurred—that is most cruel!—and yet something must tell you that I do not deserve it."

"Madam!"

"Listen to me! and may God convince you. This is a solemn hour in my existence. Since the first glance you ever cast upon me, sir—on that day when I went up to you while you were sketching the old church—since that first glance, I belonged to you. I have never loved, I shall never love any man but you. Will you take me for your wife? I am worthy of it—I swear it to you in the presence of that Heaven which is looking down upon us!"

"Dear madam—dear child—your kindness, your affection move me to the depths of my soul; in mercy, be more calm; let me retain a gleam of reason!"

"Ah! if your heart speaks, listen to it, sir! It is not with reason that I can be judged! Alas! I feel it! you still doubt me, you still doubt my past life. Oh, Heavens! that opinion of the world which I have always scorned, how it is killing me now!"

"No, madam, you are mistaken; but what could I offer you in exchange for all you wish to sacrifice for my sake—for the habits, the tastes, the pleasures of your whole life?"

"But that life inspires me with horror! You think that I would regret it? You think that some day I may again become the woman I have been, the madcap you have known?—you think so! And how can I help your believing it? And yet I know very well that I would never cause you that sorrow, nor any other—never! I have discovered in your eyes a new world I did not know—a more dignified, more lofty world, of which I had never conceived the idea—and outside of which I can no longer live. Ah! you must certainly feel that I am telling you the truth!"

"Yes, madam, you are telling me the truth—the truth of the hour—of a moment of fever and excitement; but this new world, which appears dimly to you now—this ideal world in which you desire to seek an eternal refuge against mere transient evils—would never keep all it seems to promise. Disappointment, regret, misery await you within it—and do not await you alone. I know not if there be a man gifted with a sufficiently noble mind, with a sufficiently lofty soul to make you love the new existence of which you are dreaming to preserve in the reality the almost divine character which your imagination imparts to it; but I do know that such a task, sweet as it might be, is beyond my strength; I would be insane, I would be a wretch, if I were to accept it."

"Is that your final decision? Cannot reflection alter it in any way?"

"In no way."

"Farewell then, sir—ah! unhappy woman that I am!—farewell!"

She grasped my hand, which she wrung convulsively, and then left me.

After she had disappeared, I sat down on the bench, upon which she had been seated. There, my dear Paul, my whole strength gave way. I hid my head in my hands and I wept like a child. Thank God, she did not return!

I had at last to gather all my courage in order to appear once more and for a moment in the ballroom. There was nothing to indicate that my absence had been noticed, or unfavorably commented upon. Madame de Palme was dancing and displaying a degree of gayety amounting almost to delirium. Soon after, supper was announced, and I availed myself of the general commotion attending that incident, to retire to my room.

Early this morning, I requested a private interview with Madame de Malouet. It appeared to me that my entire confidence was due to her. She heard me with profound sadness, but without manifesting any surprise.

"I had guessed," she told me, "something of the kind—I did not sleep all night. I believe that you have done your duty as a wise man and as an honest man. Yes, you have. Still, it seems very hard. Society life is detestable in this, that it creates fictitious characters and passions, unexpected situations, subtle shades, which complicate strangely the practice of duty, and obscure the straight path which ought to be always simple and easy to discover. And now you wish to leave, I suppose?"

"Certainly, madam."

"Very well; but you had better stay two or three days longer. You will thus remove from your departure the semblance of flight which, after what may have been observed, might prove somewhat ridiculous and perhaps damaging. It is a sacrifice I ask of you. Today, we are all to dine at Madame de Breuilly's; I'll undertake to excuse you. In this manner, this day at least will rest lightly upon you. Tomorrow, we'll act for the best. Day after tomorrow, you can leave."

I accepted these terms. I shall soon see you again, then, Paul. But in the meantime, how lonely and forsaken I feel! How I long to grasp your firm and loyal hand; to hear your voice tell me: "You have done right!"

CHAPTER VIII.

"I Am a Disgraced Woman."

Rozel, *October 10.*

Here I am back in my cell, my friend. Why did I ever leave it? Never has a man felt a more troubled heart beat between these cold walls, than my own wretched heart! Ah! I will not curse our poor human reason, our philosophy; are they not, after all, the noblest and best conquests of our nature? But, great Heaven! how little they amount to! What unreliable guides, and what feeble supports! Listen to a sad story: Yesterday, thanks to Madame de Malouet, I remained alone at the chateau the whole day and the whole evening. I was therefore as much at peace as it was possible for me to be. Toward midnight I heard the carriages returning, and soon after all noise ceased. It was, I think, about three o'clock in the morning when I was aroused from the species of torpor that has stood me in lieu of sleep for the past few nights, by the sound quite close to me, of a door cautiously opened or closed in the yard. I know not by what strange and sudden connection of ideas so simple an incident attracted my attention and disturbed my mind. I left abruptly the armchair in which I had been slumbering, and I went up to a window. I distinctly saw a man moving off with discreet steps in the direction of the avenue. I had no difficulty in satisfying myself that the door through which he had just passed, was that which gives access to the wing of the chateau contiguous to the library. This part of the house contains several rooms devoted to transient guests; I knew that all were vacant at this moment, unless Madame de Palme, as it often happened, had occupied for the night the lodging that was always set apart for her in that wing.

You may guess what strange thought floated across my brain. I repelled it at first as sheer madness; but remembering, within the field of my somewhat extended experience, certain facts that lent probability to that thought, I entertained it with a sort of cynical irony, and I was almost ready to admit it, as an odious but decisive denouement. The early dawn found me struggling still in this mental anguish, calling up my recollections, examining in a childish way the most minute circumstances that might tend to confirm or to banish my suspicions. Excess of fatigue, brought on at last two hours of prostration, from which I emerged with a better command of my reason. It was impossible for me to doubt the reality of the apparition that had struck my eyes during the night; but it appeared to me that I had put upon it a hasty and senseless construction, and that my ailing spirit had attributed to it the least likely explanation.

I went down at half past ten o'clock as usual. Madame de Palme was in the parlor; she must therefore have spent the night at the chateau. Nevertheless, a mere glance at her was enough to remove from my mind the very shadow of suspicion. She was talking quietly in the center of a group. She greeted me with her usual gentle smile. I felt relieved of an immense weight. I was escaping a torment of such a painful and bitter nature, that the positive impression of my previous grief, freed from the disgraceful complications with which I had for a moment thought it aggravated, appeared almost pleasant. Never had my heart rendered to this woman a more tender and more sincere homage. I was grateful to her from the bottom of my soul, for having restored purity to my wound and to my memory.

The afternoon was to be devoted to a horseback ride along the seashore. In the effusion of heart that succeeded the anxieties of the night, I yielded quite readily to the entreaties of Monsieur de Malouet, who, arguing on my approaching departure, was urging me to accompany him on this excursion. It was about two o'clock when our cavalcade, recruited as usual by a few young men of the neighborhood, marched out of the chateau's gate. We had been traveling merrily for a few minutes, and I was not the least merry of the band, when Madame de Palme suddenly came to take her place by my side.

"I am about to be guilty of a base deed," she said; "and yet, I had so strongly resolved—but I am choking!"

I looked at her; the haggard expression of her eyes and of her features suddenly struck me with terror.

"Well!" she went on, in a voice of which I shall never forget the tone, "you have willed it so! I am a disgraced woman!"

She urged at once her horse forward, leaving me crushed by this blow, the more terrible that I had wholly ceased to fear it, and that it struck me with a keen cruelty I had not even foreseen. There had indeed been in the unhappy woman's voice no trace whatever of insolent swaggering; it was the very voice of despair, a cry of heart-rending grief and timid reproach; everything that might add in my soul to the torture of a stained and shattered love, the disorder of a profound pity and an uneasy conscience.

When I had found strength enough to look around me I was surprised at my own blindness. Among Madame de Palme's most assiduous courtiers, figures one Monsieur de Mauterne, whose antipathy for me, though confined within the limits of good-breeding, often seemed to me to assume an almost hostile tinge. Monsieur de Mauterne is a man of my age, tall, blonde, with a figure more robust than elegant, and features regularly handsome, but stiff and without expression. He possesses social accomplishments, much audacity, and no wit. His bearing and his conduct during the course of that fatal ride would have informed me from the start, if I had only thought of observing them, that he believed he had the right of fearing henceforth no rivalry near Madame de Palme. He assumed frankly the leading part in all the scenes in which she participated; he overwhelmed her with attentions, affected to speak to her in a whisper, and neglected nothing, in a word, to initiate the public into the secret of his success. In that respect, he lost his trouble; the world, after exhausting its wickedness upon imaginary errors, seems thus far to refuse the evidence which vainly stares it in the face.

As to myself, my friend, it would be difficult to depict the chaos of emotions and thoughts that tossed and tumbled in my brain. The feeling that swayed me perhaps with the greatest violence, was that of hatred against that man—a feeling of implacable hatred, of eternal hatred. I was, however, more shocked and more distressed than surprised at the choice that had been made of him; he had happened in the way, and he had been taken up with a sort of indifference and of scorn, as one picks up any weapon to commit suicide with, when once the suicide has been resolved upon. As to my feelings toward her, you may guess them; not a shadow of anger, frightful sadness, tender compassion, vague remorse, and above all, passionate, furious regret. I realized at last how much I had loved her! I could scarcely understand the motives which, two days before, had appeared to me so powerful, so imperative, and which had seemed to raise between her and me an insurmountable barrier. All these obstacles of the past disappeared before the abyss of the present which seemed the only real one, the only one that was impossible to overcome, the only one that ever existed. Strange fact! I could see clearly, as clearly as I saw the sun, that the impossible, the irreparable was there, and I could not accept it, I could not submit to it. I could see that woman lost to me as irrevocably as if the grave had closed over her coffin, and I could not give her up! My mind wandered through insane projects and resolutions; I thought of picking a quarrel with Monsieur de Mauterne, and compelling him to fight on the spot. I felt that I would have crushed him! Then I thought of fleeing with her, of marrying her, of taking her with her shame, after having refused her pure! Yes, this madness tempted me! To remove it from my thoughts, I had to repeat a hundred times to myself that mutual disgust and dispair were the only fruits that could ever be expected of that union of a dishonored hand with a bloody hand. Ah; Paul, how much I did suffer!

Madame de Palme manifested during the entire course of our ride a feverish excitement which betrayed itself more particularly in reckless feats of horsemanship. I heard at intervals her loud bursts of merriment, that sounded to my ears like heart-rending wails. Once again she spoke to me as she was going by.

"I inspire you with horror, don't I?" she said.

I shook my head and dropped my eyes without replying.

We returned to the chateau at about four o'clock. I was making my way to my room when a confused tumult of voices, shrieks, and hurried steps in the vestibule chilled my heart. I went down again in all haste, and I was informed that Madame de Palme had just been taken with a nervous fit. She had been carried into the parlor. I recognized through the door the grave and gentle voice of Madame de Malouet, to which was mingled I know not what moan, like that of a sick child. I ran away. I was resolved to leave this fatal spot without further delay. Nothing could have induced me to remain a moment longer. Your letter, which had been handed to me on our return, served me as a likely pretext for my sudden departure. The friendship that binds us is well-known here. I said you needed me within twenty-four hours. I had taken care, at all hazards, to send three days before to the nearest town for a carriage and horses. In a few minutes my preparations were made; I gave orders to the driver to start ahead and wait for me at the extremity of the avenue while I was taking my leave. Monsieur de Malouet seemed to have no suspicion of the truth; the worthy old gentleman appeared quite moved as he received my thanks, and really manifested for me a singular affection out of all proportion to the brief duration of our acquaintance. I had to be scarcely less thankful to M. de Breuilly. I regret now the caricature I once gave you as the portrait of that noble heart.

Madame de Malouet insisted upon accompanying me down the avenue a few steps farther than her husband. I felt her arm trembling under mine while she was intrusting me with a few trifling errands for Paris. At the moment of parting, and as I was pressing her hand with effusion, she detained me gently:

"Well! sir," she said in a feeble voice, "God did not bless our wisdom."

"Our hearts are open to Him, madam; He must have read our sincerity; He sees how much I am suffering, and I humbly hope He may forgive me!"

"Do not doubt it—do not doubt it," she replied in a broken voice; "but she? she!—ah! poor child!"

"Have pity on her, madam. Do not forsake her. Farewell!"

I left her hastily, and I started, but instead of going direct to the town, I had myself driven along the abbey road as far as the top of the hills; I requested the coachman to go alone to the town, and to return for me tomorrow morning early at the same place. I cannot explain to you, my dear friend, the singular and irresistible fancy that I took to spend one last night in that solitude where I spent such quick and happy days, and so recently, mon Dieu!

Here I am, then, back in my cell. How cold, dark, and gloomy it seems! The sky also has gone into mourning. Since my arrival in this neighborhood, and in spite of the season, I had seen none but summer days and nights. Tonight a cold autumnal storm has burst over the valley; the wind howls among the ruins, blowing off fragments that fall heavily upon the ground. A driving rain is pattering against my windowpanes. It seems to me as if it were raining tears!

Tears! my heart is overflowing with them—and not a single one will rise to my eyes. And yet, I have prayed, I have long prayed to God—not, my friend to that untangible God whom we pursue in vain beyond the stars and the worlds, but the only true God, truly kind and helpful to suffering humanity, the God of my childhood, the God of that poor woman!

Ah! I wish to think now only of my approaching meeting with you, the day after tomorrow, dear friend, and perhaps before this letter—

Come, Paul! If you can leave your mother, come, I beseech you, come to uphold me. God's hand is upon me!

I was writing that interrupted line when, in the midst of the confused noises of the tempest, I fancied I heard the sound of a voice, of a human groan. I rushed to my window; I leaned outside to pierce the darkness, and I discovered lying upon the drenched soil a vague form, something like a white bundle. At the same time, a more distinct moan rose up to me. A gleam of the terrible truth flashed through my brain like a keen blade. I groped through the darkness as far as the door of the mill; near the threshold, stood a horse bearing a side-saddle. I ran madly around to the other side of the ruins, and within the inclosure situated beneath the window of my cell, and which still retains some traces of the former cemetery of the monks, I found the unhappy creature. She was there, sitting on an old tombstone, as if overwhelmed, shivering in all her limbs under the chilling torrent of rain which a pitiless sky was pouring without interruption over her light party-dress. I seized her two hands, trying to raise her up.

"Ah! unhappy child! what have you done!"

"Yes, most unhappy!" she murmured, in a voice as faint as a breath.

"But you are killing yourself."

"So much the better—so much the better!"

"You cannot remain there! Come!—"

I saw that she was unable to stand up alone.

"Ah! *Dieu bon! Dieu puissant!* what shall I do? What's to become of you now? What do you wish with me?"

She made no reply. She was trembling, and her teeth were chattering. I lifted her up in my arms and I carried her in. The mind works fast in such moments. No conceivable means of removing her from this valley where carriages cannot penetrate; nothing was henceforth possible to save her honor; I must only think of her life. I scaled rapidly the steps leading to my cell, and I seated her on a chair in front of the chimney in which I hastily kindled a fire; then I woke up my hosts. I gave to the miller's wife a vague and confused explanation. I know not how much of it she understood; but she is a woman, she took pity and went on bestowing upon Madame de Palme such care as was in her power. Her husband started at once on horseback, carrying to Madame de Malouet the following note from me:

> "Madam:—She is here, dying. In the name of the God of mercy, I beseech you, I implore you—come to console, come to bless her who can no longer expect words of kindness and forgiveness from any one but you in this world.
> "Pray tell Madame de Pontbrian whatever you think proper."

She was calling me. I returned to her side. I found her still seated before the fire. She had refused to be put into the bed that had been prepared for her. When she saw me—singular womanly preoccupation!—her first thought was for the coarse peasant's dress she had just exchanged for her own water-soaked and mud-stained garments. She laughed as she called my attention to it; but her laughter soon turned into convulsions which I had much difficulty in quieting.

I had placed myself close to her; she had a consuming fever, her eyes glistened. I begged her to consent to take the absolute rest which was alone suitable to her condition.

"What is the use?" she replied. "I am not ill. It is not the fever that is killing me, nor the cold, it is the thought that is burning me there;"—she touched her forehead—"it is shame—it is your scorn and your hatred; now, alas! but too well deserved!"

My heart overflowed then, Paul; I told her everything; my passion, my regrets, my remorse! I covered with kisses her trembling hands, her cold forehead, her damp hair. I poured into her poor shattered soul all the tenderness, all the pity, all the adoration a man's soul can contain! She knew now that I loved her; she could not doubt it!

She listened to me with rapture. "Now," she said, "now, I am no longer to be pitied. I have never been so happy in all my life. I did not deserve it—I have nothing further to wish—nothing further to hope—I shall not regret anything."

She fell into a slumber. Her parted lips are smiling a pure and placid smile; but she is taken at intervals with terrible spasms, and her features are becoming terribly altered. I am watching her while writing these lines.

Madame de Malouet has just arrived with her husband. I had judged her rightly! Her voice and her words were those of a mother. She had taken care to bring her physician. The patient is lying in a comfortable bed, surrounded by loving and attentive friends. I feel more easy, although she has just awakened with a fearful delirium.

Madame de Pontbrian has positively refused to come to her niece. I had judged her rightly too, the excellent Christian!

I have deemed it my duty not to set foot again in the cell which Madame de Malouet no longer leaves. The expression of M. de Malouet's countenance terrifies me, and yet he assures me that the physician has not yet pronounced.

The doctor has just come out; I have spoken to him.

"It is pneumonia," he told me, "complicated with brain fever."

"It is very serious, is it not?"

"Very serious."

"But is there any immediate danger?"

"I'll tell you that tonight. Her condition is so acute that it cannot last long. Either the crisis must abate or nature must yield."

He looked up to heaven and went off.

I know not what is going on within me, my friend—all these blows are striking me in such rapid succession. It is the lightning!

FIVE O'CLOCK P.M.

The old priest whom I have often met at the chateau has been sent for in haste. He is a friend of Madame de Malouet, a simple old man, full of charity; I dared not question him. I know not what is going on. I fear to hear, and yet my ear catches eagerly the least noises, the most insignificant sounds; a closing door, a rapid step on the stairs strikes me dumb with terror. And yet—so quick! it seems impossible!

Paul, my friend—my brother! where are you?—all is over!

An hour ago I saw the doctor and the priest coming down. Monsieur de Malouet was following them.

"Go up," he told me. "Come, courage, sir. Be a man!" I walked into the cell; Madame de Malouet had remained alone there; she was kneeling by the bedside and beckoned me to approach. I gazed upon her who was about to cease suffering. A few hours had been enough to stamp upon that lovely face all the ravages of death; but life and thought still lingered in her eyes; she recognized me at once.

"Monsieur," she began; then, after a pause: "George, I have loved you much. Forgive my having embittered your life with the memory of this sad incident!"

I fell on my knees; I tried to speak, I could not; my tears flowed hot and fast upon her hand already cold and inert as a piece of marble.

"And you, too, madam," she added; "forgive me the trouble I have given you—the grief I am causing you now."

"My child!" said the old lady, "I bless you from the bottom of my heart."

Then there was a pause, in the midst of which I suddenly heard a deep and broken breath—ah! that supreme breath, that last sob of a deadly sorrow; God also has heard it, has received it!

He has heard it—He hears also my ardent, my weeping prayer. I must believe that He does, my friend. Yes, that I may not yield at this moment to some temptation of despair, I must firmly believe in a God who loves us, who looks with compassionate eyes upon the anguish of our feeble hearts—who will deign some day to tie again with His paternal hand the knots broken by cruel death!—ah! in presence of the lifeless remains of a beloved being, what heart so withered, what brain so blighted by doubt, as not to repel forever the odious thought that these sacred words: God, Justice, Love, Immortality—are but vain syllables devoid of meaning!

Farewell, Paul. You know what there still remains for me to do. If you can come, I expect you; if not, my friend, expect me. Farewell!

CHAPTER IX.

A Challenge And Duel.

The Marquis de Malouet to Paul B——, Paris.
Chateau de Malouet. *October 20.*

Monsieur:—It has become my imperative though painful duty to relate to you the facts which have brought about the crowning disaster of which you have already been advised, by more rapid means and with such precautions as we were able to take; a disaster that completely overwhelms our souls already so cruelly tried. As you are aware, sir, a few weeks, a few days had been sufficient to enable Madame de Malouet and myself to know and appreciate your friend, to conceive for him an eternal affection soon, alas! to be changed into eternal regret. You are also aware, I know, of all the sad circumstances that preceded and led to this sad catastrophe.

Monsieur George's conduct during the melancholy days that followed the death of Madame de Palme, the depth of feeling as well as the elevation of soul which he constantly manifested had completely won our hearts over to him. I desired to send him back to you at once, sir; I wished to get him away from this sorrowful spot, I wished to take him to you myself, since a painful preoccupation detained you in Paris; but he had imposed upon himself the duty of not forsaking so soon what was left of the unhappy woman.

We had removed him to our house; we were surrounding him with attentions. He never left the chateau, except to go each day on a pious pilgrimage within a few steps. Still, his health was perceptibly failing. Day before yesterday morning, Madame de Malouet pressed him to join Monsieur de Breuilly and myself in a horseback ride. He consented, though somewhat reluctantly. We started. On the way, he strove manfully to respond to the efforts we were making to draw him into conversation and rouse him from his prostration. I saw him smile for the first time in many hours, and I began to hope that time, the strength of his soul, the attentions of friendship, might restore some calm to his memory, when, at a turn in the road, a deplorable chance brought us face to face with Monsieur de

Mauterne.

This gentleman was on horseback; two friends and two ladies made up his party. We were following the same direction, but his gait was much more rapid than ours; he passed us, saluting as he did so, and I noticed, so far as I am concerned, nothing in his manner that could attract attention. I was therefore much surprised to hear M. de Breuilly the next moment murmur between his teeth: "That is an infamous trick!" Monsieur George, who, at the moment of meeting, had become pale and turned his head slightly away, looked sharply at Monsieur de Breuilly:

"What do you mean, sir? What do you refer to?"

"I refer to the impertinence of that brainless fool!"

I appealed energetically to Monsieur de Breuilly, reproaching him with his quarrelsome disposition, and affirming that there had been no trace of defiance either in the attitude or the features of Monsieur de Mauterne when he had passed by us.

"Come, my friend," said Monsieur de Breuilly, "your eyes must have been closed—or else you must have seen, as I saw myself, that the wretch giggled as he looked at our friend. I don't know why you should wish the gentleman to suffer an insult which neither you nor I would suffer!"

These unlucky words had been scarcely uttered, when Monsieur George started his horse at a gallop.

"Are you mad?" I said to De Breuilly, who was trying to detain me; "and what means such an invention?"

"My friend," he replied, "it was necessary to divert that boy's mind at any cost."

I shrugged my shoulders. I freed myself from him and dashed after Monsieur George; but, being better mounted than myself, he had already gained considerable advance. I was still a hundred paces behind him when he overtook Monsieur de Mauterne, who had stopped on hearing him coming. It seemed to me that they were exchanging a few words, and almost at once I saw Monsieur George's whip lashing several times, and with a sort of fury, Monsieur de Mauterne's face. We barely arrived in time, Monsieur de Breuilly and myself, to prevent that scene from assuming an odious character of brutality.

A meeting having unfortunately become inevitable between the parties, we took with us the two friends who accompanied Mauterne, Messieurs de Quiroy and Astley, the latter an Englishman. Monsieur George had preceded us to the chateau. The choice of weapons belonged without any possible doubt to our adversary. Nevertheless, having noticed that his seconds seemed to hesitate with a sort of indifference, or perhaps of circumspection between swords and pistols, I thought that we might, with a little good management, influence their decisions in the direction least unfavorable to us. We went, therefore, Monsieur de Breuilly and I, to consult Monsieur George on the subject. He pronounced at once in favor of swords.

"But," remarked Monsieur de Breuilly, "you are a very good pistol-shot. I have seen you at work. Are you certain to be a better swordsman? Do not deceive yourself; this will be a mortal combat."

"I am satisfied of that," he replied, with a smile; "but I am particularly anxious for swords, if at all possible."

After the expression of so formal a wish, we could but esteem ourselves fortunate in obtaining the choice of arms, and the meeting was settled for the next morning at nine o'clock.

During the remainder of the day, Monsieur George manifested an ease of mind, and even at intervals a certain gayety, at which we were quite surprised, and which Madame de Malouet, in particular, was at a loss to understand. My poor wife of course had been left in ignorance of these recent events.

At ten o'clock he retired, and I could still see a light through his window two hours later. Impelled by my earnest affection and I know not what vague anxiety was haunting me, I entered his room at about midnight; I found him very calm; he had been writing and was just sealing up a few envelopes.

"There!" he said, handing me the papers. "Now the worst is over, and I am going to sleep the sleep of the just."

I thought it best to offer him a few more technical suggestions on the handling of the weapon he was soon to use. He listened to me without much attention, and suddenly extending his arm:

"Feel my pulse," he said.

I did so, and ascertained that his calm and his cheerfulness were neither affected nor feverish.

"In such a condition," he added, "if a man is killed it is because he is willing to be. Good-night, my dear sir!" Whereupon I left him.

Yesterday morning, at half past eight, we repaired, Monsieur George, Monsieur de Breuilly, and myself, to an unfrequented path situated about half way between Mauterne and Malouet, and which had been selected for the dueling-ground. Our adversary arrived almost immediately after, accompanied by Messieurs de Quiroy and Astley. The nature of the insult admitted of no attempt at conciliation. We had therefore to proceed at once to the fight.

Scarcely had Monsieur George placed himself in position, when we became convinced of his complete inexperience in the use of the sword. Monsieur de Breuilly cast upon me a look of stupor. However, after the blades had been crossed, there was a semblance of fight and of defense; but at the third pass, Monsieur George fell pierced through the chest.

I threw myself upon him; he was already in the grasp of death. Nevertheless he pressed my hand feebly, smiled once more, then gave vent, with his last breath, to his last thought, which was for you, sir:

"Tell Paul that I love him, that I forbid him seeking to avenge me, and that I die—happy." He expired.

I shall not attempt, sir, to add anything to this narrative. It has already been too long and too painful to me; but I deemed this faithful and minute account due to you. I had reason to believe, besides, that your friendship would like to follow to the last instant that existence which was so justly dear to you. Now you know all, you have understood all, even what I have left unsaid.

He lies in peace by her side. You will doubtless come, dear sir. We expect you. We shall mingle our tears over those two beloved beings, both kind and charming, both crushed by passion and seized by death with relentless rapidity in the midst of the pleasantest scenes of life.

THE END

THE SPHINX;

OR,

"JULIA DE TRECŒUR."

CHAPTER I.

"A Baleful Affection."

All those who, like ourselves, knew Raoul de Trecœur during his early youth, believed that he was destined to great fame. He had received quite remarkable gifts from nature; there are left from him two or three sketches and a few hundred verses that promised a master; but he was very rich, and had been very badly brought up; he soon gave himself up to dilettanteism. A perfect stranger, like most men of his generation, to the sentiment of duty, he permitted himself to be recklessly carried away by his instincts, which, fortunately for others, were more ardent than hurtful. Therefore was he generally pitied when he died, in the flower of his age, for having loved and enjoyed immoderately everything that he thought pleasant.

The poor fellow, they said, never did any harm but to himself; which, in point of fact, was not the exact truth. Trecœur had married, at the age of twenty-five, his cousin, Clotilde Andree de Pers, a modest and graceful person who had of the world nothing but its elegance. Madame de Trecœur had lived with her husband in an atmosphere of unhealthy storms, where she felt out of place, and, as it were, degraded. He tormented her with his remorse almost as much as he did with his faults. He looked upon her, and justly, as an angel, and wept at her feet when he had betrayed her, lamenting that he was unworthy of her; that he was the victim of his temperament, and that he had been born in a faithless age. He threatened once to kill himself in his wife's boudoir if she did not forgive him; she forgave him, of course. All this dramatic action disturbed Clotilde in her resigned existence. She would have preferred that her misery should have been more quiet and less declamatory.

All the friends of her husband had been in love with her, and had built great hopes upon her forlorn condition, but unfaithful husbands do not always make guilty wives. The reverse is rather more frequently the case, so little is this poor world submitted to the rules of logic. In short, Madame de Trecœur, after her husband's death was left forlorn, exhausted, and broken down, but spotless.

From this melancholy union, a daughter had been born, named Julia, and whom her father, notwithstanding all Clotilde's efforts of resistance, had spoilt to excess. Monsieur de Trecœur's idolatry for his daughter was well-known, and the world, with its habitual weakness of judgment, forgave him readily his scandalous existence in consideration of that merit, which is not always a great one. It is not, indeed, a very difficult matter to love one's children; it is sufficient for that not to be a monster. The love that one has for them is not in itself a virtue; it is a passion which, like all others, may be good or bad, as one is its master or its slave. It may even be thought that there is no passion which may be more than this one, pregnant with good or with evil.

Julia seemed splendidly gifted; but her ardent and precocious disposition had been developed, thanks to the paternal education, as in the primeval forest, wholly at random. She was small in person, dark and pale, lithe and slender, with large blue eyes full of fire, unruly black hair, and superbly arched eyebrows. Her habitual air was reserved and haughty; nevertheless she laid aside, at home, these majestic appearances to frolic on the carpet. She played games of her own invention. She translated her history lessons into little dramas interspersed with speeches to the people, dialogues, music, and particularly chariot races. In spite of her serious countenance, she could be very funny at times, and made cruel fun of those she did not like.

She manifested for her father a passionate predilection, singularly mitigated by the sentiments of tender pity which her mother's unhappiness inspired in her youthful heart. She saw her weep often; she would then throw herself upon the floor, curled up at her feet, and there remain for hours, motionless and dumb, looking at her with moist eyes, and drinking from time to time a tear from her cheek.

She had apparently caught, as many children do, some echoes of the domestic woes. Doubtless her quick intellect appreciated her father's wrongdoings; but her father—that handsome gentleman, so witty, generous, and wild—she worshiped him; she was proud to be his daughter; she palpitated with joy when he clasped her to his heart. She could neither judge him nor blame him; he was a superior being. She contented herself with pitying and consoling, as best she could, that gentle and charming creature who was her mother, and who suffered.

Within the circle of Madame de Trecœur's acquaintances, Julia simply passed for a little plague. The dear madames, as she called them, who formed the ornament of her mother's Thursdays, related with bitterness to each other the scenes of comical imitation with which the child followed their entrance and their departure. The men considered themselves fortunate when they did not carry off a bit of paper or silk on the back of their coats. All this amused Monsieur de Trecœur extremely. When his daughter performed with half a dozen chairs some of those Olympian races that knocked every piano in the neighborhood out of tune—.

"Julia!" he would exclaim, "you don't make noise enough. Smash a vase."

And a vase she did smash; whereupon her father kissed her with enthusiasm.

This method of education assumed a graver character as the child grew older. Her father's affection became shaded with a species of gallantry. He took her with him to the Bois, to the races, to the theater. She had not a fancy that he did not anticipate and gratify. At thirteen years of age, she had her horse, her groom, and a carriage bearing her monogram. Already ill, and having perhaps a presentiment of his death, the unfortunate man overwhelmed that beloved daughter with the tokens of his baleful affection. He was thus blunting all her tastes by too precocious satiety, as if he had intended to leave her no taste save for the forbidden fruit.

Julia wept over him with furious transports, and preserved for his memory a fervid worship. She had a private room which she filled with the portraits of her father and with a thousand personal souvenirs, around which she kept up flowers.

Madame de Trecœur, like the greater number of young girls who marry their cousins, had married very young. She was left a widow at twenty-eight, and her mother, the Baroness de Pers, who was still living, and who was even of the liveliest, was not long in suggesting discreetly to her the propriety of a second marriage. After having exhausted the practical and, in fact, quite sensible reasons that seemed to urge that course, the baroness then came down to the sentimental reasons:

"In good faith, my poor child," she said, "you have not had, up too this time, your just share of happiness in this world. I would not speak ill of your husband, since he is dead; but, *entre nous*, he was a horrid brute. Mon Dieu! charming at times, I grant you,—since I have been caught myself—like all worthless scamps! but in fact, beastly, beastly! Well, certainly, I shall not undertake to say that marriage is ever a state of perfect bliss; nevertheless it is the best thing that has been imagined up to this time, to enjoy life decently among respectable people. You are in the flower of your age—you are quite good-looking, quite—and, by the way, it will do you no harm to wear your skirts a little higher up behind, with a proper sort of bustle; for you don't even know what they wear now, my poor pet. Here, look! It's horrible, I know; but what can we do? we must not attract attention. In short, what I meant to tell you is that you still have all that is necessary, and even more than is necessary, to fix a husband—if indeed there are any that can be fixed, which I hope is the case—otherwise, we should have to despair wholly of Providence, if it did not have some compensation in store for us after all our trials. It is already a manifest sign of its kindness that you should have recovered your *embonpoint*, my darling! Kiss your mother. Come, now, when is our pretty little woman going to be married?"

There was no maternal exaggeration whatever in the compliments which the baroness was addressing to Clotilde. All Paris looked upon her with the same eyes as her mother. She had never been so attractive as now, and she had always been infinitely so. Her person, reposed in the peace of her mourning, had then the bright lustre of a fine fruit, ripe and fresh. Her black eyes full of timid tenderness, her pure brow crowned with splendid and lifelike braids, her shoulders of rosy marble, her particular grace of a young matron, at once handsome, loving, and chaste—all that, joined to a spotless reputation and to sixty thousand francs a year, could not fail to bring forward more than one pretender. And indeed they sprang up in legions. Reason, and public opinion itself, which had done full justice to her husband and to herself, were both urging her to a second wedding. Her own private feelings, whatever might be their natural delicacy, did not seem likely to prove an obstacle, for there was nothing in her heart that was not true. She had been faithful to her husband, she had shed sincere and bitter tears over that wretched companion of her youth; but he had exhausted and worn out her affection, and without ever joining her mother in her posthumous recriminations against Monsieur de Trecœur, she felt that she had no further duty to fulfill toward him but that of prayer.

She had, however, been for many months a widow, and she still continued to oppose to the solicitations of the baroness, a resistance of which the latter sought in vain to ascertain the mysterious cause. One day she fancied she had discovered it.

"Confess the truth," she said to her; "you are afraid to cause some annoyance to Julia. Now, if that is so, my dear daughter, it is pure folly. You cannot have any serious scruple on that score. Julia will be very rich in her own right, and will have no need of your fortune. She will herself marry in three or four years (much pleasure do I wish her husband, by the way!); and see a little in what a nice situation you will find yourself then! But, mon Dieu! are we never going to be done with them? After the father, here is the daughter now! Eh! mon Dieu! let her erect chapels with her father's portraits and spurs as much as she likes—that's her business; I am certainly not the one to enter into competition with her. But she must at least allow us to live in peace! What! You could not dispose of your person without her leave! Then if you are her slave, my dear child, show me the door at once! You could not do anything more agreeable to her for she cannot bear the sight of me, your daughter! And then, after all, in all candor, what possible objection can she have to your getting married again? A step-father is not a step-mother; it's quite another thing. Eh! mon Dieu! her step-father will be charming to her—all men will be charming to her; I predict her that; she may feel easy about it! Now, will you admit that it is the true cause of your hesitation?"

"I assure you that it is not, mother," said Clotilde.

"I assure you that it is, my daughter. Well, come; would you like me to speak to Julia, to try and reason with her? I would prefer giving her a good whipping; however—!"

"Poor, dear mother," rejoined Clotilde, "must I then tell you everything?"

She came to kneel down in front of the baroness.

"By all means, daughter; tell me everything, but don't make me cry, I beg of you! Is what you have to tell very sad?"

"Not very gay."

"Mon Dieu! But no matter; go on."

"In the first place, mother, I must confess that I would personally feel no scruple in marrying again—"

"I should think not! That would be carrying it just a little too far!"

"As to Julia—whom I adore, who loves me sincerely, and who loves you very much too, whatever you may say—"

"Satisfied of the contrary," said the baroness. "But no matter; proceed."

"As to Julia, I have more confidence than you have in her good sense and in her good heart; notwithstanding the exalted affection she has preserved for her father, I am sure that she would understand, that she would respect my determination, and that she would not love me one whit the less, especially if her step-father did not happen to be personally objectionable to her; for you are aware of the extreme violence of her sympathies and of her antipathies—"

"I am aware of it!" said the baroness, bitterly. "Well, you must give her a list of your gentlemen friends, the dear little thing, and she will pick out her own choice for you."

"There is no need of that, good mother," said Clotilde. "The choice has already been made by the mainly interested party, and I am certain that it would not be disagreeable to Julia."

"Well, then, my darling, everything is for the best."

"Alas! no. I am going to tell you something that covers me with confusion. Among all the men we know, the only one who—the only one I like, in fact, is also the only one who has never been in love with me."

"He must be a savage, then! he cannot but be a savage. But who is he?"

"I have told you, dear mother, the only one of our friends who is not in love with me—"

"Bah! who is that? Your cousin Pierre?"

"No, but you are not—"

"Monsieur de Lucan!" exclaimed the baroness. "It could not fail to be so! The very flower of the flock! Mon Dieu, my darling, how very similar our tastes are, both of us! He is charming, your Lucan, he is charming. Kiss me, dear—don't look any farther, don't look any farther; he is positively just the man for us."

"But, mother, since he does not want me!"

"Good! he does not want you now! What nonsense! what do you know about it? Did you ask him? Besides, it is impossible, my darling; you were made for each other in all eternity. He is charming, *distingue*, well-bred, rich, intelligent, everything, in a word—everything."

"Everything, mother, except in love with me."

The baroness exclaiming anew against such a very unlikely thing, Clotilde exposed to her eyes a series of facts and particulars which left no room for illusions. The dismayed mother was compelled to resign herself to the painful conviction that there really was in the world a man of sufficiently bad taste not to be in love with her daughter, and that this man unfortunately was Monsieur de Lucan.

She returned slowly to her residence, meditating on the way upon that strange mystery the explanation of which, however, she was not long to wait.

CHAPTER II.

Two Fast Friends.

George-Rene de Lucan was an intimate friend of the Count Pierre de Moras, Clotilde's cousin. They had been companions in boyhood, in youth, in travels, and even in battle; for, chance having led them to the United States at the outbreak of the war of the rebellion, they had deemed it a favorable opportunity to receive the baptism of fire. Their friendship had become still more sternly tempered in the midst of these dangers of warfare sustained fraternally far from their own country. That friendship had had, moreover, for a long time, a character of rare confidence, delicacy, and strength. They entertained the highest esteem for each other, and their mutual confidence was not misplaced. They, however, bore no resemblance whatever to each other. Pierre de Moras was of tall stature, blonde as a Scandinavian, handsome and strong as a lion, but as a good-natured lion. Lucan was dark, slender, elegant and grave. There was in his cold and gentle accent, in his very bearing, a certain grace mingled with authority, that was both imposing and charming.

They were not less dissimilar in a moral point of view; the former a jolly companion, an absolute and settled skeptic, the careless possessor of a danseuse; the latter always agitated despite his outer calm, romantic, passionate, tormented with love and theology. Pierre de Moras, on their return from America, had presented Lucan to his cousin Clotilde, and from that moment there were at least two points upon which they agreed perfectly; profound esteem for Clotilde, and deep-seated antipathy for her husband.

They appreciated, however, each in his own way, Monsieur de Trecœur's character and conduct. For the Count Pierre, Trecœur was simply a mischievous being; in Monsieur de Lucan's eyes, he was a criminal.

"Why criminal?" Pierre said. "Is it his fault if he was born with the eternal flames on the marrow of his bones? I admit that I feel quite disposed to break his head when I see Clotilde's eyes red; but I would not feel any more angry about it, than if I were crushing a serpent under my heel. Since it is his nature, the poor man can't help it."

"That little system of yours would simply suppress all merit, all will, all liberty; in a word, the whole moral world. If we are not the masters of our own passions, at least to a great extent, and if, on the contrary, it is our passions that fatally control us; if a man is necessarily good or bad, honest or a knave, loyal or a traitor, at the mercy of his instincts, tell me, if you please, why you honor me with your esteem and your friendship? I have no right to them any more than any one else, any more than Trecœur himself."

"I beg your pardon, my friend," said Pierre gravely; "in the vegetable world I prefer a rose to a thistle; in the moral world, I prefer you to Trecœur. You were born a gallant fellow; I rejoice at it, and I make the best of it."

"Well, *mon cher*, you are laboring under a complete mistake," rejoined Lucan. "I was born, on the contrary, with the most detestable instincts, with the germ of all vices."

"Like Socrates?"

"Like Socrates, exactly. And if my father had not chastised me in time, if my mother had not been a saint, finally, if I had not myself placed, with the utmost energy, my will at the service of my conscience, I would be today, a faithless and lawless scoundrel."

"But nothing proves that you will not turn out a scoundrel one of these days, my dear friend. There is no one but may become a scoundrel at the proper time. Everything depends upon the extent and strength of the temptation. Whatever may be your instinct of honor and dignity, are you yourself quite sure never to meet with a temptation sufficiently powerful to overcome your principles? Can you not conceive, for instance, some circumstance in which you might love a woman enough to commit a crime?"

"No," said Lucan; "do you?"

"I!—I deserve no credit. I have no passions. It is extremely mortifying, but I have none. I was born to be an exemplary man. You remember my childhood; I was a little model. Now I am a big model, that's all the difference—and it does not cost me any effort whatever. Shall we go and see Clotilde?"

"Let us go!"

And they went to Clotilde's, very worthy herself of the friend-ship of these two excellent fellows.

There they were received with marked consideration, even by Mademoiselle Julia, who seemed to feel, to a certain degree, the pres-tige of these superior natures. Both had, moreover, in their manners and language an elegant correctness that apparently satisfied the child's delicate taste and her artistic instincts.

During the early period of her mourning, Julia's disposition had assumed a somewhat shy and somber cast; when her mother received visitors, she left the parlor abruptly, and went to lock herself up in her own room, not, however, without manifesting toward the indis-creet guests a haughty displeasure. Cousin Pierre and his friend had alone the privilege of a kindly greeting; she even deigned to leave her apartment and come and join them at her mother's side when she knew that they were there.

Clotilde had therefore good reasons to believe that her prefer-ence for Monsieur de Lucan would obtain her daughter's approba-tion; she unfortunately had better ones still to doubt that Monsieur de Lucan's disposition corresponded with her own. Not only, indeed, had he always maintained toward her the terms of the most reserved friendship, but, since she had been a widow, that reserve had become perceptibly aggravated. Lucan's visits became fewer and briefer; he even seemed to take particular care in avoiding all occa-sions of finding himself alone with Clotilde, as if he had penetrated her secret feelings, and had affected to discourage them. Such were the sadly significant symptoms which Clotilde had communicated in confidence to her mother.

On the very day when the baroness was receiving this unpleasant information at the residence of her daughter, a conversation was taking place upon the same subject between the Count de Moras and George de Lucan, in the latter's apartment. They had taken together, during the forenoon a ride through the Bois, and Lucan had shown himself even more silent than usual. At the moment of parting:

"*Apropos*, Pierre," he said, "I am tired of Paris; I am going to travel."

"Going to travel! Where on earth?"

"I am going to Sweden. I have always wished to see Sweden."

"What a singular thing! Will you be gone long?"

"Two or three months."

"When do you expect to leave?"

"Tomorrow."

"Alone?"

"Entirely so. I'll see you again at the club, tonight, won't I?"

The strange reserve of this dialogue left upon the mind of Monsieur de Moras an impression of surprise and uneasiness. He was unable to withstand the feeling, and two hours later he returned to Lucan's. As he went in, preparations for traveling greeted his eyes on all sides. Lucan was engaged writing in his study.

"Now, my dear fellow!" said the count to him, "if I am impertinent, say so frankly and at once; but this sudden and hurried voyage doesn't look like anything. Seriously, what is the matter? Are you going to fight a duel outside the frontier?":

"Bah! In that case I should take you with me; you know that very well."

"A woman, then?"

"Yes," said Lucan dryly.

"Excuse my importunity, and good-by."

"I have wounded your feelings, dear friend?" said Lucan, detaining him.

"Yes," said the count, "I certainly do not pretend to enter into your secrets; but I do not absolutely understand the tone of restraint, and almost of hostility, in which you are answering me on the subject of this journey. It is not, moreover, the first symptoms of that nature that strike and grieve me; for some time past, I find you visibly embarrassed in your intercourse with me; it seems as though I were in your way and my friendship were a burden to you, and the cruel idea has occurred to my mind that this journey is merely a way of putting an end to it."

"Mon Dieu!" murmured Lucan. "Well, then," he went on with evident agitation in his voice, "I must tell you the whole truth; I hoped that you would have guessed it—it is so simple. Your cousin, Clotilde, has now been a widow for nearly two years; that, I believe, is the term consecrated by custom to the mourning of a husband. I am aware of your feelings toward her; you may now marry her, and you will be perfectly right in doing so. Nothing seems to me more just, more natural, more worthy of her and of yourself. I beg to assure you that my friendship for you shall remain faithful and entire, but I trust you will not object to my keeping away for a short time. That's all."

Monsieur de Moras seemed to have infinite difficulty in comprehending the meaning of this speech; he remained for several seconds after Lucan had ceased to speak, with wondering countenance and fixed gaze, as if trying to find the solution of a riddle; then rising abruptly and grasping both Lucan's hands:

"Ah! that's kind of you, that is!" he said with grave emotion.

And after another cordial grasp, he added gayly:

"But if you expect to stay in Sweden until I have married Clotilde, you may begin building and even planting there, for I swear to you that you shall stay long enough for either purpose."

"Is it possible that you do not love her?" said Lucan in a half whisper.

"I love her very much, on the contrary; I appreciate her, I admire her; but she is a sister to me, purely a sister. The most delightful thing about it, *mon cher*, is that it has always been my dream to have you and Clotilde marry; only you seemed to be so cold, so little attentive, so rebellious, particularly lately. Mon Dieu! how pale you are, George!"

The final result of this conversation was that Monsieur de Lucan, instead of starting for Sweden, called a little later to see the Baroness de Pers, to whom he exposed his aspirations, and who thought herself, as she listened to him, in the midst of an enchanting dream. She had, however, beneath her frivolous manners too profound a sentiment of her own dignity and that of her daughter, to manifest in the presence of Monsieur de Lucan the joy that overwhelmed her. Whatever desire she might have felt of clasping immediately upon her heart this ideal son-in-law, she deferred that satisfaction and contented herself with expressing to him her personal sympathy. Appreciating, however, Monsieur de Lucan's just impatience, she advised him to call that very evening upon Madame de Trecœur, of whose personal sentiments she was herself ignorant, but who could not fail to meet his advances with the esteem and the consideration due to a man of his merit and standing. Being left alone, the baroness gave way to her feelings in a soliloquy mingled with tears; she, however, purposely omitted to notify Clotilde, preferring with her maternal taste to leave her the whole enjoyment of that surprise.

The heart of woman is an organ infinitely more delicate than ours. The constant exercise which they give it develops within it finer and subtler faculties than the dry masculine intellect can ever hope to possess; that accounts for their presentiments, less rare and more certain than ours. It seems as though their sensibility, always strained and vibrating, might be warned by mysterious currents of divine instinct, and that it guesses even before it can understand. Clotilde, when Monsieur de Lucan was announced, was, as it were, struck by one of these secret electric thrills, and in spite of all the objections to the contrary that beset her mind, she felt that she was loved, and that she was on the point of being told so. She sat down in her great armchair, drawing up with both hands the silk of her dress, with the gesture of a bird that flaps its wings. Lucan's visible agitation further enlightened and delighted her. In such men, armed with powerful but sternly restrained passions, accustomed to control their own feelings, intrepid and calm, agitation is either frightful or charming.

After informing her—which was entirely useless—that his visit to her was one of unusual importance:

"Madam," he added, "the request I am about to address you demands, I know, a well-matured answer. I will therefore beg of you not to give that answer today, the more so that it would indeed be painful to me to hear it from your own lips if it where not a favorable one."

"Mon Dieu! monsieur!" said Clotilde faintly.

"The baroness, your mother, madam, whom I had the pleasure of seeing during the day, was kind enough to hold out some encouragement to me—in a measure—and to permit me to hope that you might entertain some esteem for me, or at least that you had no prejudice against me. As to myself madam, I—mon Dieu! I love you, in a word, and I cannot imagine a greater happiness in the world than that which I would hold at your hands. You have known me for a long time; I have nothing to tell you concerning myself. And now, I shall wait."

She detained him with a sign of her hand, and tried to speak; but her eyes filled with tears. She hid her face in her hands, and she murmured:

"Excuse me! I have been so rarely happy! I don't know what it is!"

Lucan got gently down upon his knees before her, and when their eyes met, their two hearts suddenly filled like two cups.

"Speak, my friend!" she resumed. "Tell me again that you love me. I was so far from thinking it! And why is it? And since when?"

He explained to her his mistake, his painful struggle between his love for her and his friendship for Pierre.

"Poor Pierre!" said Clotilde, "what an excellent fellow. But no, really!"

Then he made her smile by telling her what mortal terror and apprehension had taken possession of his soul at the moment when he was asking her to decide upon his fate; she had seemed too him, more than ever, at that moment, a lovely and sainted creature, and so much above him, that his pretension of being loved by her, of becoming her husband, had suddenly appeared to him as a pretension almost sacrilegious.

"Oh, mon Dieu!" she said, "what an opinion have you formed of me, then? It's frightful! On the contrary, I thought myself too simple, too commonplace for you; I thought that you must be fond of romantic passions, of great adventures; you have somewhat the appearance of it, and even the reputation; and I am so far from being a woman of that kind!"

Upon that slight invitation, he told her two events of his past life which had been full of trite excitement, and had afforded him nothing but disappointment and disgust. Never, however, before having met her, had the thought of marrying occurred to him; in the matter of love as in the matter of friendship, he had always had the imagination taken up with a certain ideal, somewhat romantic indeed, and he had feared never to find it in marriage. He might have looked for it elsewhere, in great adventures, as she said; but he loved order and dignity in life, and he had the misfortune of being unable to live at war with his own conscience. Such had been his agitated youth.

"You ask me," he went on with effusion, "why I love you. I love you because you alone have succeeded in harmonizing within my heart two sentiments which had hitherto struggled for its mastery at the cost of fearful anguish; honor and passion. Never before knowing you had I yielded to one of these sentiments without being made wretched by the other. They always seemed, irreconcilable to me. Never had I yielded to passion without remorse; never had I resisted it without regret. Whether weak or strong, I have always been unhappy and tortured. You alone made me understand that I could love at once with all the ardor and all the dignity of my soul; and I selected you because you are affectionate and you are sincere; because you are handsome and you are pure; because there are embodied in you both duty and rapture, love and respect, intoxication and peace. Such is the woman, such is the angel you are to me, Clotilde."

She listened to him half reclining, drinking in his words and manifesting in her eyes a sort of celestial surprise.

But it seems—who has not experienced it?—that human happiness cannot touch certain heights without drawing the lightning upon itself. Clotilde in the midst of her ecstasy shuddered suddenly and started to her feet. She had just heard a smothered cry, followed by the dull sound of a falling body. She ran, opened the door, and in the center of the adjoining room saw Julia stretched upon the floor.

She supposed that the child at the moment of entering the parlor had overheard some of their words, and then the thought of seeing her father's place occupied by another, striking her thus without warning, had stirred to its very depths that passionate young soul. Clotilde followed her into her room, where she had her carried, and expressed the wish of remaining alone with her. While lavishing upon her cares, caresses, and kisses, it was not without fearful anguish that she awaited her daughter's first glance. That glance fell upon her at first with vague uncertainty, then with a sort of wild stupor. The child pushed her away, gently; she was trying to collect her ideas, and as the expression of her thought grew firmer in her eyes, her mother could plainly read in them a violent strife of opposing feelings.

"I beg of you, I beseech you, my darling daughter," murmured

Clotilde, whose tears fell drop by drop upon the pale visage of the child.

Suddenly Julia seized her by the neck, drew her down upon herself, and kissing her passionately:

"You have hurt me much," she said, "oh! very much more than you can imagine; but I love you. I love you a great deal; I shall, I must always, I assure you."

She burst into sobs, and both wept long, closely clasped to each other.

In the meantime Monsieur de Lucan had deemed it advisable to send for the Baroness de Pers, whom he was entertaining in the parlor. The baroness on hearing what was going on had manifested more agitation than surprise.

"Mon Dieu!" she exclaimed, "I expected it fully, my dear sir. I did not tell you anything about it, because we hadn't got so far yet; but I expected it fully. That child will kill my daughter. She will finish what her father has so well begun; for it is purely a miracle if my daughter, after all she has suffered, has been able to recover as far as you see. I must leave them together. I am not going in there. Oh, mon Dieu! I am not going in there! In the first place, I would be afraid of annoying my daughter, and besides, that would be entirely out of my character."

"How old is Mademoiselle Julia?" inquired Lucan, who retained under these painful circumstances his quiet courtesy.

"Why, she is almost fifteen, and I'm not sorry for it, by the way, for, *entre nous*, we may reasonably hope to get honestly rid of her within a year or two. Oh! she will have no trouble in getting married, no trouble whatever, you may be sure. In the first place she is rich, and then, after all, she is a pretty monster, there is no gainsaying that, and there is no lack of men who admire that style."

Clotilde joined them at last. Whatever might have been her inward emotion, she appeared calm, having nothing theatrical in her ways. She replied simply, in a low and gentle voice, to her mother's feverish questions; she remained convinced that this misfortune would not have happened, if she could have herself informed Julia, with some precautions, of the event which chance had abruptly revealed to her. Addressing then a sad smile to Monsieur de Lucan:

"These family difficulties, sir," she said to him, "could not have formed a part of your anticipations, and I should deem it quite natural were they to lead to some modification of your plans.":

An expressive anxiety became depicted upon Lucan's features. "If you ask me to restore to you your freedom," he said, "I cannot but comply; if it is your delicacy alone that has spoken, I beg to assure you that you are still dearer to me since I have seen you suffer on my account, and suffer with so much dignity."

She held out her hand, which he seized, bowing low at the same time.

"I shall love your daughter so much," he said, "that she will forgive me."

"Yes, I hope so," said Clotilde; "nevertheless, she wishes to enter a convent for a few months, and I have consented."

Her voice trembled and her eyes became moist.

"Excuse me, sir," she added; "I have no right as yet to make you participate to such an extent in my sorrows. May I beg of you to leave me alone with my mother?"

Lucan murmured a few words of respect, and withdrew. It was quite true, as he had said, that Clotilde was dearer to him than ever. Nothing had inspired him with such a lofty idea of the moral worth of that woman as her attitude during that trying evening. Stricken in the midst of her flight of happiness, she had fallen without a cry, without a groan, striving to hide her wound; she had manifested in his presence that exquisite modesty in suffering so rare among her sex. He was the more grateful to her for it, that he was deeply averse to those pathetic and turbulent demonstrations which most women never fail to eagerly exhibit on every occasion, when they are indeed kind enough not to bring them about.

CHAPTER III.

Julia's Champion.

Monsieur de Lucan had been Clotilde's husband for several months when the rumor spread among society that Mademoiselle de Trecœur, formerly known as such an incarnate little devil, was about taking the vail in the convent of the Faubourg Saint Germain, to which she had withdrawn before her mother's marriage. That rumor was well founded. Julia had endured at first with some difficulty the discipline and the observances to which the simple boarders of the establishment were themselves bound to submit; then she had been gradually taken with a pious fervor, the excesses of which they had been compelled to moderate. She had begged her mother not to put an obstacle to the irresistible inclination which she felt for a religious life, and Clotilde had with difficulty obtained permission that she should adjourn her resolution until the accomplishment of her sixteenth year.

Madame de Lucan's relations with her daughter since her marriage had been of a singular character. She came almost daily to visit her, and always received the liveliest manifestations of affection at her hands; but on two points, and those the most sensitive, the young girl had remained inflexible; she had never consented either to return to the maternal roof, nor to see her mother's husband.

She had even remained for a long time without making the slightest allusion to Clotilde's altered situation, which she affected to ignore. One day, at last, feeling the intolerable torture of such a reserve, she made up her mind, and fixing her flashing eyes upon her mother:

"Well, are you happy at last?" she said.

"How can I be," said Clotilde, "since you hate the man I love?"

"I hate no one," replied Julia, dryly. "How is your husband?"

From that moment she inquired regularly after Monsieur de Lucan in a tone of polite indifference; but she never uttered without hesitation and evident discomfort the name of the man who had taken her father's place.

In the meantime she had reached her sixteenth year. Her mother's promise had been formal. Julia was henceforth free to follow her vocation, and she was preparing for it with an impatient ardor that edified the good ladies of the convent. Madame de Lucan expressing, one morning, in the presence of her mother and her husband the anxiety that oppressed her heart during these last days of respite:

"As to me, my daughter," said the baroness, "I must confess that I am urging with all my wishes and prayers the moment which you seem to dread. The life you have been leading since your marriage has nothing human about it; but what forms its principal torment, is the constant struggle which you have to sustain against that child's obstinacy. Well, when she has become a nun, there will no longer be any struggle; the situation will be clearer; and note that you will not be in reality any more separated than you are now, since the house is not a cloister; I would just as lief it were, myself; but it is not. And then, why oppose a vocation which I really look upon as providential? In the interest of the child herself, you should congratulate yourself upon the resolution she has taken; I appeal to your husband to say if that is not so. Come, let me ask you, my dear sir, what could be expected of such an organization, if she were once let loose upon the world? Why! she would be a dangerous character for society! You know what a head she has! a volcano! And pray observe, my friend, that at this present moment she is a perfect odalisk. You have not seen her for some time; you cannot imagine how she has developed. I, who enjoy the treat of seeing her twice a week, can positively assure you that she is a perfect odalisk, and besides, divinely dressed. In fact, she is so well made! you might throw a window-curtain over her with a pitchfork, and she would look as if she were just coming out of Worth's! There, ask Pierre what he thinks about it, he who has the honor of being admitted to her good graces!"

Monsieur de Moras, who was coming in at that very moment, shared, indeed, with a very limited number of friends of the family, the privilege of accompanying Clotilde occasionally on her visits to Julia's convent.

"Well, my good Pierre," resumed the baroness, "we were speaking of Julia, and I was telling my son-in-law that it was really quite fortunate that she was willing to become a saint, because otherwise she would certainly set Paris on fire!"

"Because?" asked the count.

"Because she is beautiful as Sin!"

"Undoubtedly she is quite good-looking," said the count somewhat coldly.

The baroness having gone out on some errands with Clotilde, Monsieur de Moras remained alone with Lucan.

"It really seems to me," he said to the latter, "that our poor Julia is being very harshly treated."

"In what way?"

"Her grandmother speaks of her as of a perverse creature! And what fault do they find with her after all? Her worship of her father's memory! It is excessive, I grant; but filial piety, even when exaggerated, is not a vice, that I know of. Her sentiments are exalted; what does it matter if they are generous? Is that a reason why she should be devoted to the infernal divinities and thrust out of the way to be forgotten?"

"But you are very strange, my friend, I assure you," said Lucan. "What is the matter with you? whom do you mean to blame? You are certainly aware that Julia proposes taking the vail wholly of her own accord; that her mother is distressed about it, and that she has spared no effort to dissuade her from that step. As to myself, I have no reason whatever to be fond of her; she has caused and is still causing me much grief; but you know well enough that I have ever been ready to greet her as my daughter, if she had deigned to return to us."

"Oh! I accuse neither her mother nor yourself, of course; it is the baroness who irritates me; she is unnatural! Julia is her grandchild after all, and she rejoices—she positively rejoices—at the prospect of seeing her a nun!"

"*Ma foi*, I declare to you that I am not far from rejoicing too. The situation is too painful for Clotilde; it must be brought to an end; and as I see no other possible solution—"

"But I beg your pardon; there might be another."

"And which?"

"She might marry."

"How likely! and marry—whom, pray?"

The count approached nearer to Lucan, looked him straight in the face, and smiling with some embarrassment:

"Me!" he said.

"Repeat that!" said Lucan.

"*Mon cher*," rejoined the count, "you see that I am as red as a peony; spare me. I have wished for a long time to broach that delicate question to you, but my courage has failed me; since I have found it, at last, don't deprive me of it."

"My dear friend," said Lucan, "allow me to recover a little first, for I am falling from the clouds. What! you are in love with Julia?"

"To an extraordinary degree, my friend."

"No! there is something under that; you have discovered this means of drawing us together, and you wish to sacrifice yourself for the peace of the family."

"I swear to you that I am not thinking in the least of the peace of the family; I am thinking wholly of my own, which is very much disturbed, for I love that child with an energy of feeling that I never knew before. If I don't marry her, I shall never console myself for the rest of my life."

"To that extent?" said Lucan, dumfounded.

"It is a terrible thing, *mon cher*," rejoined Monsieur de Moras. "I am absolutely in love; when she looks at me, when I touch her hand, when her dress rustles against me, I feel, as it were, a philter running through my veins. I had heard of emotions of that kind, but I had never felt them. I must confess that they delight me; but at the same time they distress me, for I cannot conceal the fact to myself that there are a thousand chances against one that my passion will not be reciprocated, and it really seems as though my heart should wear mourning for it as long as it shall beat."

"What an adventure!" said Lucan, who had recovered all his gravity. "That is a very serious matter; very annoying."

He walked a few steps about the parlor, absorbed in thoughts that seemed of a rather somber character.

"Is Julia aware of your sentiments?" he said, suddenly.

"Most certainly not; I would not have taken the liberty of informing her of them without first speaking to you. Will you be kind enough to act as my ambassador to her mother?"

"Why, yes, with pleasure," said Lucan, with a shade of hesitation that did not escape his friend.

"You think that is useless, don't you?" said the count with a forced smile.

"Useless—why so?"

"In the first place, it is very late."

"It is somewhat late, no doubt. Things have gone very far; but I have never had much confidence in the stability of Julia's ideas of her vocation. Besides, in these restless imaginations, the sincerest resolutions of today become readily the dislikes of the morrow."

"But you doubt that—that I should succeed in pleasing her?"

"Why should you not please her? You are more than good-looking. You are thirty-two years old; she is sixteen. You are a little richer than she is. All that does very well."

"Well, then, why do you hesitate to serve me?"

"I do not hesitate to serve you; only I see you very much in love; you are not accustomed to it, and I fear that a condition of things so novel for you might be urging you somewhat hastily to such a grave determination as marriage. A wife is not a mistress. In short, before taking an irrevocable step I would beg of you to think well and further over it."

"My good friend," said the count, "I do not wish, and I believe quite sincerely that I cannot, do so. You know my ideas. Genuine passions always have the best of it, and I am not quite sure that honor itself is a very effective argument against them. As to setting up reason against them, it is worse than folly. Besides, come, Lucan, what is there so unreasonable in the simple fact of marrying a person I love? I don't see that it is absolutely necessary for a man not to love his wife—Well! can I rely upon you?"

"Completely so," said Lucan, taking his hand. "I raised my objections; now I am wholly at your service. I shall speak to Clotilde in a moment. She is going to see her daughter this afternoon. Come and dine with us tonight; but summon up all your courage, for, after all, success is very uncertain."

Monsieur de Lucan found it no difficult task to gain the cause of Monsieur de Moras with Clotilde. After hearing him, not, however, without interrupting him more than once with exclamations of surprise:

"Mon Dieu!" she replied, "that would be an ideal! Not only would that marriage put an end to projects that break my heart, but it offers all the conditions of happiness that I can possibly think of for my daughter; and furthermore, the friendship that binds you to Pierre would naturally, some day, bring about a *rapprochement* between his wife and yourself. All that would be too fortunate; but how could we hope for such a complete and sudden revolution in Julia's ideas? She will not even allow me to deliver my message to the end."

She left, palpitating with anxiety. She found Julia alone in her room, trying on before a mirror her novice's dress; the vail that was to conceal her luxuriant hair was laid upon the bed; she was simply dressed in a long, white woolen tunic, whose folds she was engaged in adjusting.

She blushed when she saw her mother come in; then with an insipient laugh:

"Cymodocea in the circus, isn't it, mother?"

Clotilde made no answer; she had joined her hands in a supplicating attitude, and wept as she looked at her. Julia was moved by that mute sorrow; two tears rolled from her eyes, and she threw her arms around her mother's neck; then, taking a seat by her side:

"What can I do?" she said; "I, too, feel some regret at heart, for, after all, I was fond of life; but aside from my vocation, which I believe quite real, I am yielding to a positive necessity. There is no other existence possible for me but that one. I know very well—it's my own fault; I have been somewhat foolish—I should not have left you in the first place, or at least, I should have returned to your house immediately after your marriage. Now, after months, and even years, is it possible, I ask you? In the first place, I would die with shame. Can you imagine me in the presence of your husband? What sort of countenance could I put on? And then, he must fairly detest me, the bent must be firmly taken in his mind. Finally, I should be in all respects terribly in your way!"

"But, my dear child, no one hates you; you would be received with transports of joy, like the prodigal child. If you deem it too painful to return to my home—if you fear to find or to bring trouble there with you—God knows how mistaken you are on this point! but still, if you do fear it, is that a reason why you should bury yourself alive and break my heart? Could you not return into the world without returning to my own house, and without having to face all those difficulties that frighten you? There would be a very simple way of doing that, you know!"

"What is it?" said Julia quietly; "to marry?"

"Undoubtedly," said Clotilde, shaking her head gently and lowering her voice.

"But, mon Dieu! mother, what possible chance is there of such a thing? Suppose I were willing—and I am far from it—I know no one, no one knows me."

"There is some one," rejoined Clotilde, with increasing timidity; "some one whom you know perfectly well, and who—who adores you."

Julia opened her eyes wide with a pensive and surprised expression, and after a brief pause of reflection:

"Pierre?" she said.

"Yes," murmured Clotilde, pale with anxiety.

Julia's eyebrows became slightly contracted; she raised her head and remained for a few seconds with her eyes fixed upon the ceiling; then, with a slight shrug of her shoulders:

"Why not?" she said gravely. "I would as soon have him as any one else!"

Clotilde uttered a feeble cry, and grasping both her daughter's hands:

"You consent?" she said; "you really consent? And may I take your answer to him?"

"Yes, but you had better change the text of it," said Julia, laughing.

"Oh! my darling, darling dear!" exclaimed Clotilde, covering Julia's hands with kisses; "but repeat again that it is all true—that by tomorrow you will not have changed your mind."

"I will not change my mind," said Julia, firmly, in her grave and musical voice.

She meditated for a moment and then resumed:

"Really, he loves me, that big fellow!"

"Like a madman."

"Poor man! And he is waiting for an answer?"

"With the utmost anxiety."

"Well, go and quiet his fears. We will take up the subject again tomorrow. I require to put a little order in my thoughts after all this confusion and excitement, you understand; but you may rest easy. I have decided."

When Madame de Lucan returned home, Pierre de Moras was waiting for her in the parlor. He turned very pale when he saw her.

"Pierre!" she said, all panting still, "come and kiss me, you are my son! Respectfully, if you please, respectfully!" she added laughingly as he lifted her up and clasped her to his heart.

A little later, he had the gratification of treating in the same manner the Baroness de Pers, who had been sent for in haste.

"My dear friend," said the baroness, "I am delighted, really delighted, but you are choking me—yes, yes, it is all for the best, my dear fellow—but you are literally choking me, I tell you! Reserve yourself, my friend, reserve yourself!—The dear child! that's quite nice of her, quite nice! In point of fact, she has a heart of gold! And then she has good taste, too, for you are very handsome yourself, very handsome, *mon cher*, very handsome! To be perfectly candid, I always had an idea that, at the moment of cutting off her hair, she would think the matter over. And she has such beautiful hair, the poor child!"

And the baroness melted into tears; then addressing the count in the midst of her sobs:

"You'll not be very unhappy either, by the way; she is a goddess!"

Monsieur de Lucan, though deeply moved by this family tableau, and above all, by Clotilde's joy, took more coolly that unexpected event. Besides that he did not generally show himself very demonstrative in public, he was sad and anxious at heart. The future prospects of this marriage seemed extremely uncertain to him, and in his profound friendship for the count he felt alarmed. He had not ventured, through a sentiment of delicate reserve toward Julia, upon telling him all he thought of her character and disposition. He strove to banish from his mind as partial and unjust the opinion he had formed of her; but still he could not help remembering the terrible child he had known once, at times wild as a hurricane, at others pensive and wrapped in gloomy reserve; he tried to imagine her such as she had been described to him since; tall, handsome, ascetic; then he fancied her suddenly casting her vail to the winds, like one of the fantastic nuns in "Robert le Diable," and returning swift-footed into the world; of all these various impressions he composed, in spite of himself, a figure of Chimera and Sphinx, which he found very difficult to connect with the idea of domestic happiness.

They discussed in the family circle, during the whole evening, the complications which might arise from that marriage project, and the means of avoiding them. Monsieur de Lucan entered into all these details with the utmost good grace, and declared that he would lend himself heartily, for his own part, to all the arrangements which his daughter-in-law might wish. That precaution was not destined to be useless.

Early the next morning, Clotilde returned to the convent. Julia, after listening with slightly ironical nonchalance to the account which her mother gave her of the transports and the joy of her intended, assumed a more serious air.

"And your husband," she said, "what does he think of it?"

"He is delighted, as we all are."

"I am going to ask you a single question: does he expect to be present at our wedding?"

"That will be just as you like."

"Listen, good little mother, and don't grieve in advance. I know very well that sooner or later, this marriage must be the means of bringing us all together; but let me have a little time to become accustomed to the idea. Grant me a few months so that the old Julia may be forgotten, and I may forget her myself—you will; say, won't you?"

"Anything you please," said Clotilde, with a sigh.

"I beg of you. Tell him that I beg of him, too."

"I'll tell him; but do you know that Pierre is here?"

"Ah! *mon Dieu!* and where did you leave him?"

"I left him in the garden."

"In the garden! how imprudent, mother! why, the ladies are going to tear him to pieces—like Orpheus, for you may well believe that he is not in the odor of sanctity here."

Monsieur de Moras was sent for at once, and he came up in all haste. Julia began laughing as he appeared at the door, which facilitated his entree. She had several times, during their interview, fits of that nervous laughter which is so useful to women in trying circumstances. Deprived of that resource, Monsieur de Moras contented himself with kissing the beautiful hands of his cousin, and was otherwise generally wanting in eloquence; but his handsome and manly features were resplendent, and his large blue eyes were moist with gratified affection. He appeared to leave a favorable impression.

"I had never considered him in that light," said Julia to her mother; "he is very handsome—he will make a splendid-looking husband."

The marriage took place three months later, privately and without any display. The Count de Moras and his youthful bride left for Italy the same evening.

Monsieur de Lucan had left Paris two or three weeks before, and had taken up his quarters in an old family residence at the very extremity of Normandy, where Clotilde hastened to join him immediately after Julia's departure.

CHAPTER IV.

A Grewsome Abode.

Vastville, the patrimonial domain of the Lucan family, is situated a short distance from the sea, on the west coast of the Norman Finisterre. It is a manor with high roof and wrought-iron balconies, which dates from the time of Louis XIII., and which has taken the place of the old castle, a few ruins of which still serve to ornament the park. It is concealed in a thickly shaded depression of the soil, and a long avenue of antique elms precedes it. The aspect of it is singularly retired and melancholy, owing to the dense woods that surround it on all sides. This wooded thicket marks, on this point of the peninsula, the last effort of the vigorous vegetation of Normandy. As soon as its edge has been crossed, the view extends suddenly and without obstacle over the vast moors which form the triangular plateau of the Cape La Hague; fields of furze and heather, stone fences without cement, here and there a cross of granite, on the right and on the left the distant undulations of the ocean—such is the severe but grand landscape that is suddenly unfolded to the eyes beneath the unobstructed light of the heavens.

Monsieur de Lucan was born in Vastville. The poetic reminiscences of childhood mingled in his imagination with the natural poetry of that site, and made it dear to him. Under pretext of hunting, he came on a pilgrimage to it every year. Since his marriage only, he had given up that habit of the heart, in order not to leave Clotilde, who was detained in Paris by her daughter; but it had been agreed upon that they would go and bury themselves in that retreat for a season as soon as they had recovered their liberty. Clotilde only knew Vastville from her husband's enthusiastic descriptions; she loved it on his representations, and it was for her, in advance, an enchanted spot. Nevertheless, when the carriage that brought her from the station entered, at nightfall, among the wooded hills, in the gloomy avenue that led up to the chateau, she felt an impression as of cold.

"Mon Dieu! my dear," she said, laughingly, "your chateau is a perfect castle of Udolpho!"

Lucan excused his chateau as best he could, and protested, more-over, that he was ready to leave it the very next day, if she were not better pleased with its appearance after sunrise.

It was not long before she became passionately fond of it. Her happiness, hitherto so constrained, blossomed freely for the first time in that solitude, and shed upon it a charming light. She even expressed the wish of spending the winter and waiting there for Julia, who was to return to France in the course of the following year. Lucan offered some slight opposition to that project, which appeared to him rather over-heroic for a Parisian, but ended by adopting it, too happy himself to harbor the romance of his love in that romantic spot. He began, however, taxing his ingenuity to attenuate what there might be too austere in that abode, by opening relations with some of the neighbors for Clotilde's benefit, and by procuring her, at intervals, her mother's society. Madame de Pers was kind enough to lend herself to that combination, although the country was generally repulsive to her, and Vastville in particular had in her eyes a sinister character. She pretended that she heard at night noises in the walls and moans in the woods. She slept with one eye open and two candles burning. The magnificent cliffs that bordered the coast a short distance off, and which they tried to make her admire, caused her a painful sensation.

"Very fine!" she said, "very wild! quite wild! But it makes me sick; I feel as though I were on top of the towers of Notre Dame! Besides, my children, love beautifies everything, and I understand your trans-ports perfectly. As to myself, you must excuse me if I do not share them. I can never go into ecstasies over such a country as this. I am as fond of the country as any one, but this is not the country—it is the desert, Arabia Petrœa, I know not what. And as to your chateau, my dear friend—I am sorry to tell you so: it has a savor of crime. Look well, and you'll see that a murder has been committed in it."

"Why, no, my dear madam," replied Lucan laughingly, "I know perfectly the history of my family, and I can guarantee you—"

"Rest assured, my friend, that some one has been killed in it—in old times. You know how little they troubled themselves about those things formerly!"

Julia's letters to her mother were frequent. It was a regular journal of travels written helter-skelter, with a striking originality of style, in which the vivacity of the impressions was corrected by that shade of haughty irony which was a peculiarity of the writer. Julia spoke rather briefly of her husband, but always in pleasant terms. There was generally a rapid and kindly postscript addressed to Monsieur de Lucan.

Monsieur de Moras was more chary of descriptions. He seemed to see no one but his wife in Italy. He extolled her beauty, still further enhanced, he said, by the contact of all those marvels of art with which she was becoming impregnated; he praised her extraordinary taste, her intelligence, and even her good disposition. In this latter respect, she was extremely matured, and he found her almost too staid and too grave for her age. These particulars delighted Clotilde, and finished instilling into her heart a peace she had never yet enjoyed.

The count's letters were not less reassuring for the future than the present. He did not think it necessary, he said, to urge Julia on the subject of her reconciliation with her step-father; but he felt that she was quite ready for it. He was, besides, preparing her more and more for it by conversing habitually with her of the old friendship that united him to Monsieur de Lucan, of their past life, of their travels, of the perils they had braved together. Not only did Julia hear these narratives without revolt, but she often solicited them, as if she had regretted her prejudices, and had sought good reasons to forget them.

"Come, Pylades, speak to me of Orestes!" she would say.

After having spent the whole winter season and part of the spring in Italy, Monsieur and Madame de Moras visited Switzerland, announcing their intention of sojourning there until the middle of summer. The thought occurred to Monsieur and Madame de Lucan to go and join them there, and thus abruptly bring about a reconciliation that seemed henceforth to be but a mere matter of form. Clotilde was preparing to submit that project to her daughter when she received, one beautiful May morning, the following letter dated from Paris:

"Beloved Mother:—'No more Switzerland!' too much Switzerland! Here I am; don't disturb yourself. I know how much you are enjoying yourself at Vastville. We'll go and join you there one of these fine mornings, and we'll all come home together in the autumn. I only ask of you a few days to look after our future establishment here.

"We are at the Grand Hotel. I did not choose to stop at your house, for all sorts of reasons, nor at my grandmother's, who, however, insisted very kindly upon our doing so: ·

"'Oh! mon Dieu! my dear children—that must not be—in a hotel! why, that is not proper. You cannot remain in a hotel! come and stay with me. mon Dieu! you'll be very uncomfortable. You'll be camping out, as it were. I don't even know how I'll manage to give you anything to eat, for my cook is sick abed, and that stupid coachman of mine, by the way, has a stye on his eye! But why not let people know you were coming? You fall upon me like two flowerpots from a window! It's incredible! You are in good health, my friend? I need not ask you. It shows plainly enough. And you, my beautiful pet? Why! it is the sun; the sun itself. Hide yourself—you are dazzling my eyes! Have you any luggage? Well, we'll just put it in the parlor; it can't be helped. And as to yourselves, I'll give you my own room. I'll engage a housekeeper and hire a driver from some livery stable. You'll not be in my way at all, not at all, not at all!'

"In short, we did not accept.

"But the explanation of this sudden return! Here it is:

"'Are you not tired of Switzerland, my dear?' I asked of my husband.

"'I am tired of Switzerland,' replied that faithful echo.

"'Suppose we go away, then?'

"And away we went.

"Glad and moved to the bottom of my soul at the thought of soon kissing you,
Julia.

"P.S.—I beg Monsieur de Lucan not to intimidate me."

The days that followed were delightfully busy for Clotilde. She herself unpacked the parcels that constantly kept coming, and put the contents away with her own maternal hands. She unfolded and folded again, she caressed those skirts, those waists of fine and perfumed linen, which were already to her like a part of her daughter's person. Lucan, a little jealous, surprised her meditating lovingly over these pretty things. She went to the stables to see Julia's horse, which had followed soon after the boxes; she gave him lumps of sugar and chatted with him. She filled with flowers and verdant foliage the apartments set apart for the young couple.

This fever of happiness soon came to its happy termination. About a week after her arrival in Paris, Julia wrote to her mother that they expected, her husband and herself, to leave that evening, and that they would be in Cherbourg the next morning. Clotilde prepared, of course, to go and meet them with her carriage. Monsieur de Lucan, after duly conferring with her on the subject, thought best not to accompany her. He feared that he might interfere with the first emotions of the return, and yet, not wishing that Julia should attribute his absence to a lack of attention, he resolved to go and meet the travelers on horseback.

CHAPTER V.

Father and Step-Daughter.

It was on one of the first days of June. Clotilde had left early in the morning, fresh and radiant as the dawn. Two hours later, Lucan mounted his horse and started at a walk. The roads are lovely in Normandy at this season. The hawthorn hedges perfume the country, and sprinkle here and there the edges of the road with their rosy snow. A profusion of fresh verdure, dotted with wild flowers, covers the face of the ditches. All that, under the gay morning sun, is a feast for the eyes. M. de Lucan, however, greatly contrary to his custom, bestowed but very slight attention upon the spectacle of that smiling nature. He was preoccupied, to a degree that surprised himself, with his coming meeting with his step-daughter. Julia had been such a besetting thought in his mind that he had retained of her an exaggerated impression. He strove in vain to restore her to her natural proportions, which were, after all, only those of a child, formerly a naughty child, now a prodigal child. He had become accustomed to invest her, in his imagination, with a mysterious importance and a sort of fatal power, of which he found it difficult to strip her. He laughed and felt irritated at his own weakness; but he experienced an agitation mingled with curiosity and vague uneasiness, at the moment of beholding face to face that sphinx whose shadow had so long disturbed his life, and who now came in person to sit at his fireside.

An open barouche, decked with parasols, appeared at the summit of a hill; Lucan saw a head leaning and a handkerchief waving outside the carriage; he urged at once his horse to a gallop. Almost at the same instant the carriage stopped, and a young woman jumped lightly upon the road; she turned around to address a few words to her traveling-companions, and advanced alone toward Lucan. Not wishing to be outdone in politeness, he alighted also, handed his horse to the groom who followed him, and started with cheerful alacrity in the direction of the young woman, whom he did not recognize, but who was evidently Julia. She was coming toward him without haste, with a sliding walk, rocking gently her flexible figure. As she drew near, she threw off her vail with a rapid motion of her hand, and Lucan was enabled to find again upon that youthful face, in those large and slightly clouded eyes, and the pure and stretching arch of the eyebrows, some features of the child he had known.

When Julia's glance met that of Lucan, her pale complexion became suffused with a purple blush.

He bowed very low to her, and with a smile full of affectionate grace:

"Welcome!" he said.

"Thank you, sir," said Julia, in a voice whose grave and melodious suavity struck Lucan; "friends, are we not?" And she held out both her hands to him with charming resolution.

He drew her gently to himself to kiss her; but thinking that he felt a slight resistance in the suddenly stiffening arms of his stepdaughter, he contented himself with kissing her wrist just above her glove. Then affecting to look at her with a polite admiration, which, however, was perfectly sincere:

"I really feel," he said, laughingly, "like asking you to whom I have the honor of speaking."

"You find me grown?" she said, showing her dazzling teeth.

"Surprisingly so," said Lucan; "most surprisingly. I understand Pierre perfectly now."

"Poor Pierre!" said Julia; "he is so fond of you. Don't let us keep him waiting any longer, if you please."

They started in the direction of the carriage, in front of which Monsieur de Moras was awaiting them, and while walking side by side:

"What a lovely country!" resumed Julia. "And the sea quite near?"

"Quite near."

"We'll take a ride on horseback after breakfast, will we not?"

"Quite willingly; but you must be horribly fatigued, my dear child. Excuse me! my dear—? By the way, how do you wish me to call you?"

"Call me madam. I was such a bad child!"

And she broke forth into a roll of that sudden, graceful, but somewhat equivocal laughter that was habitual with her. Then raising her voice:

"You may come, Pierre; your friend is my friend now!"

She left the two men shaking hands cordially, and exchanging the usual greetings, jumped into the carriage, and resuming her seat at her mother's side:

"Mother," she said, kissing her at the same time, "the meeting came off very well—didn't it, Monsieur de Lucan?"

"Very well, indeed," said Lucan, laughingly, "except some minor details."

"Oh! you are too hard to please, sir!" said Julia, drawing her wrappings around her.

The next moment Monsieur de Lucan was cantering by the carriage door, while the three travelers inside were indulging in one of those expansive talks that usually follow the happy solution of a dreaded crisis. Clotilde, henceforth in the full possession of all her affections, was fairly soaring in the ethereal blue.

"You are too handsome, mother," said Julia. "With such a big girl as I am, it is a positive crime!"

And she kissed her again.

Lucan, while participating in the conversation and doing to Julia the honors of the landscape, was trying to sum up within himself his impressions of the ceremony which had just taken place. Upon the whole he thought, as did his step-daughter, that it had come off very well, although it was not quite perfection. Perfection would have been to find in Julia a plain and unaffected woman, who would have simply thrown herself in her step-father's arms and laughed with him at her spoilt child's escapade; but he had never expected Julia's manners to be quite as frank and open as that. She had done in the present circumstances all that could be expected of a nature like hers; she had shown herself graciously friendly; she had, it is true, imparted to this first interview a certain solemn and dramatic turn. She was romantic, and as Lucan was tolerably so himself, this whim of hers had not proved unpleasant to him.

He had been, moreover, agreeably surprised at the beauty of Madame de Moras, which was indeed striking. The severe regularity of her features, the deep luster of her blue eyes fringed with long black lashes, the exquisite harmony of her form were not her only, nor indeed her principal attractions; she owed her rare and personal charm to a sort of strange grace mingled with flexibility and strength, that lent enchantment to her every motion. She had in the play of her countenance, in her step, in her gestures, the sovereign ease of a woman who does not feel a single weak point in her beauty, and who moves, grows, and blossoms with all the freedom of a child in his cradle or a fallow deer in the forest. Made as she was, she had no difficulty in dressing well; the simplest costumes fitted her person with an elegant precision that caused the Baroness de Pers to say in her inaccurate though expressive language:

"A pair of kid gloves would be enough to dress her with."

During that same day and those that followed, Julia conquered new titles to Monsieur de Lucan's good graces, by manifesting a strong liking for the chateau of Vastville and the surrounding sites. The chateau pleased her for its romantic style, its old-fashioned garden ornamented with yews and evergreens, the lonely avenues of the park, and its melancholy woods scattered with ruins. She went into ecstasies at the sight of the vast heather plains lashed by the ocean winds, the trees with twisted and convulsive tops, the tall granite cliffs worn by the everlasting waves.

"All that," she said, laughingly, "has a great deal of character;" and as she had a great deal of it herself, she felt in her element. She had found the home of her dreams, she was happy.

Her mother, to whom she paid up in passionate effusions all arrearages of tenderness, was still more so.

The greater part of the day was spent riding about on horseback. After dinner, Julia, with that joyous and somewhat feverish spirit that animated her, related her travels, parodying in a good-natured manner her own enthusiasm and her husband's relative indifference in presence of the masterpieces of antique art. She illustrated these recollections with scenes of mimicry in which she displayed the skill of a fairy, the imagination of an artist, and sometimes the broad humor of a low comedian. In a turn of the hand, with a flower, a bit of silk, a sheet of paper, she composed a Neapolitan, Roman, or Sicilian headdress. She performed scenes from ballets or operas, pushing back the train of her dress with a tragic sweep of her foot, and accentuating strongly the commonplace exclamations of Italian lyricism:

"Oh, Ciel! Crudel! Perfido! Oh, dio! Perdona!"

Or else, kneeling on an armchair, she imitated the voice and manner of a preacher she had heard in Rome, and who did not seem to have sufficiently edified her.

Through all these various performances she never lost a particle of her grace, and her most comical attitudes retained a certain elegance.

After all these frolics she would resume her expression of a listless queen. Beneath the charm of the life and prestige of this brilliant nature, Monsieur de Lucan readily forgave Julia the caprices and peculiarities of which she was lavishly prodigal, especially toward her step-father. She showed herself generally with him what she had been at the start; friendly and polite, with a shade of haughty irony; but she had strong inequalities of temper. Lucan surprised sometimes her gaze riveted upon him with a painful and almost fierce expression. One day she repelled with sullen rudeness the hand he offered to assist her in alighting from her horse or in climbing over a fence. She seemed to avoid every occasion of finding herself alone with him, and when she could not escape a *tête-à-tête* of a few moments, she manifested either restless irritation or mocking impertinence. Lucan fancied she reproached herself sometimes with belying too much her former sentiments, and that she thought she owed it to herself to give them from time to time a token of fidelity. He was grateful to her, however, for reserving for himself alone these equivocal manifestations, and for not troubling her mother with them. Upon the whole he attached but a slight importance to these symptoms. If there still was in the affectionate manifestations of his step-daughter something of a struggle and an effort, it was on the part of that haughty nature an excusable feature, a last resistance, which he flattered himself soon to remove by multiplying his delicate attentions toward her.

Some two weeks after Julia's arrival, there was a ball given by the Marchioness de Boisfresnay, in her chateau of Boisfresnay, which is situated two or three miles from Vastville. Monsieur and Madame de Lucan were on pleasant visiting-terms with the marchioness. They went to that ball with Julia and her husband, the gentlemen in the coupe, the ladies, on account of their dresses, occupying the carriage alone. Toward midnight, Clotilde took her husband aside, and pointing to her daughter, who was waltzing in the adjoining parlor with a naval officer:

"Hush! my dear," she said; "I have a frightful headache, and Pierre is fairly bored to death; but we have not the courage to take Julia away so early. Do you wish to make yourself very agreeable? You'll bring her home, and we will start now, Pierre and myself; we'll leave you the carriage."

"Very well, dear," said Lucan, "run off, then."

Clotilde and Monsieur de Moras slipped away at once.

A moment later Julia, cleaving her way scornfully through the throng that parted before her as before an angel of light, raised her superb brow and made a sign to Lucan.

"I don't see mother," she said.

Lucan informed her in a few words of the arrangement which had just been settled upon. A sudden flash darted across Julia's eyes; her brows became contracted; she shrugged her shoulders slightly without replying, and returned into the ballroom, waltzing through the crowd with the same tranquil insolence. She betook herself again to the arm of a naval officer, and seemed to enjoy whirling in all her splendor. And indeed her ball-dress added a strange luster to her beauty. Her shoulders and throat, emerging from her dress with a sort of chaste indifference, retained even in the animation of the dance the cold and lustrous purity of marble.

Lucan asked her to waltz with him; she hesitated, but having consulted her memory, she discovered that she had not yet exhausted the list of naval officers who had swooped down in squadrons upon that rich prey. At the end of an hour she got tired of being admired and called for the carriage. As she was draping herself in her wrappings in the vestibule, her step-father volunteered his services.

"No! I beg of you," she said, impatiently; "men don't know—don't know at all!"

Then she threw herself in the carriage with a wearied look. However, as the horses were starting:

"Smoke, sir," she said with a better grace.

Lucan thanked her for the permission, but without availing himself of it; then, while making all his little arrangements of neighborly comfort:

"You were remarkably handsome tonight, my dear child!" he said.

"Monsieur," said Julia, in a nonchalant but affirmative tone, "I forbid you to think me handsome, and I forbid you to call me 'my dear child!'"

"As you please," said Lucan. "Well, then, you are not handsome, you are not dear to me, and you are not a child."

"As for being a child, no!" she said, energetically.

She wound her vail around her head, crossed her arms over her bosom, and settled herself in her corner, where a stray moonbeam came occasionally to play over her whiteness.

"May I sleep?" she asked.

"Why, most certainly! Shall I close the window?"

"If you please. My flowers will not incommode you?"

"Not in the least."

After a pause:

"Monsieur de Lucan?" resumed Julia.

"Dear madam?"

"Do explain to me in what consist the usages of society; for there are things which I do not understand. Is it admissible—is it proper to allow a woman of my age and a gentleman of yours to return from a ball, *tête-à-tête*, at two o'clock in the morning?"

"But," said Lucan, not without a certain gravity, "I am not a gentleman; I am your mother's husband."

"Ah! that is true; of course, you are my mother's husband!" she said, emphasizing these words in a ringing voice, which caused Lucan to fear some explosion.

But, appearing to overcome a violent emotion, she went on in an almost cheerful tone:

"Yes, you are my mother's husband; and what is more, you are, according to my notion, a very bad husband for my mother."

"According to your notion!" said Lucan, quietly. "And why so?"

"Because you are not at all suited to her."

"Have you consulted your mother on that subject, my dear

madam? It seems to me that she must be a better judge of it than yourself."

"I need not consult her. It is enough to see you both together. My mother is an angelic creature, whereas you;—no!"

"What am I, then?"

"A romantic, restless man—the very reverse, in fact. Sooner or later, you'll betray her."

"Never!" said Lucan, somewhat sternly.

"Are you quite sure of that, sir?" said Julia, riveting her gaze upon him from the depths of her hood.

"Dear madam," replied Monsieur de Lucan, "you were asking me, a moment since, to explain to you what was proper and what was improper; well, it is improper that we should take, you your mother, and I my wife, as the text for a jest of that kind, and consequently, it is proper that we should drop the subject."

She hushed, remained motionless and closed her eyes. In the course of a minute or two, Lucan saw a tear fall down her long eyelashes and roll over her cheek.

"Mon Dieu! my child," he said, "I have wounded your feelings! Allow me to tender you my sincere apologies."

"Keep your apologies to yourself!" she said, in a hoarse voice, opening her eyes wide at the same time. "I have no need of your apologies any more than of your lessons! Your lessons! What have I done to deserve such a humiliation? I cannot understand. What is there more innocent than my words, and what do you expect me to tell you? Is it my fault if I am here alone with you! if I am compelled to speak to you?—if I know not what to say? Why am I exposed to such things? Why ask me more than I can do? It is presuming too much on my strength! It is enough—it is a thousand times too much already—to be compelled to act such a comedy as I am compelled to act every day. God knows I am tired of it!"

Lucan found it difficult to overcome the painful surprise that had seized him.

"Julia," he said at last, "you were kind enough to tell me that we were friends; I believed you. Is it not true, then?"

"No!"

After launching that word with somber energy, she wrapped up her head and face in her hood and vail, and remained during the rest of the way plunged into a silence which Monsieur de Lucan did not attempt to disturb.

CHAPTER VI.

A Disillusion.

After a few hours of painful sleep, Monsieur de Lucan rose the next day, his brain laden with cares.

The resumption of hostilities, which had been clearly signified to him foreboded surely fresh troubles for his peace and fresh anguish for Clotilde's happiness. Was he, then, about returning to those odious agitations which had so long harassed his existence, and this time without any hopes of escape? How, indeed, was it possible not to despair of that untamable nature which age and reason, which so much attention and affection had left unmoved in her prejudices and her hatred? How was it possible to understand, and, above all, ever to overcome the quixotic sentiment, or rather the mania which had taken possession of that concentrated soul, and which was smoldering in it, ever ready to break forth in furious outbursts?

Clotilde and Julia had not yet made their appearance. Lucan went to take a walk in the garden, to breathe once more the peace of his beloved solitude, pending the anticipated storms. At the extremity of an alley of evergreens, he discovered the Count de Moras, his arm resting on the pedestal of an old statue, and his eyes fixed on the ground.

Monsieur de Moras had never been a dreamer, but since his arrival at the chateau, he had, on more than one occasion, manifested to Lucan a melancholy state of mind quite foreign to his natural disposition. Lucan had felt alarmed; nevertheless, as he did not himself like any one to intrude upon his confidence, he had abstained from questioning him.

They shook hands as they met.

"You came home late last night?" inquired the count.

"At about three o'clock."

"Oh! *povero! Apropos*, thanks for your kindness to Julia. How did she behave to you?"

"Why—well enough," said Lucan—"a little peculiar, as usual."

"Oh! peculiar of course!"

He smiled rather sadly, took Monsieur de Lucan's arm, and leading him through the meandering paths of the garden:

"*Voyons, mon cher,*" he said in a suppressed voice, "between you and me, what is Julia?"

"How, my friend?"

"Yes, what sort of a woman is my wife? If you know, do tell me, I beg of you."

"Excuse me, but it is the very question I would like to ask of you myself."

"Of me?" said the count. "But I have not the slightest idea. She is a Sphinx, a riddle, the solution of which escapes me completely. She both charms and frightens me. She is peculiar, you said? She is more than that; she is fantastic. She is not of this world. I know not whom or what I have married. You remember that cold and beautiful creature in the Arabian tales who rose at night to go and feast in the graveyard. It's absurd, but she reminds me of that."

The count's troubled look, the constrained laugh with which he accompanied his words, moved Lucan deeply.

"So, then," said the latter, "you are unhappy?"

"It is impossible to be more so," replied the count, pressing his hand hard. "I adore her, and I am jealous—without knowing of whom and of what! She does not love me—and yet she loves some one—she must love some one! How can I doubt it? Look at her; she is the very embodiment of passion; the fire of passion overflows in her words, in her looks, in the blood of her veins! And near me, she is as cold as the statue upon a tomb!"

"Frankly, *mon cher,*" said Lucan, "you seem to exaggerate your disasters greatly. In reality they seem to amount to very little. In the first place, you are seriously in love for the first time in your life, I think; you had heard a great deal said about love, about passion, and perhaps you were expecting of them excessive wonders. In the second place, I must beg you to observe that very young women are rarely very passionate. The sort of coolness of which you complain is therefore quite easy to explain without the intervention of anything supernatural. Young women, I repeat, are generally idealists; their love has no substance. You ask of whom or of what you should be jealous? Be jealous, then, of all those vague and romantic aspirations that torment youthful imaginations; be jealous of the wind, of the tempest, of the barren moors, of the rugged cliffs, of my old manor, of my words and of my ruins—for Julia adores all that. Be jealous, above all, of that ardent worship she has avowed to her father's memory, and which still absorbs her—I have lately had a proof of the fact—the keenest of her passion."

"You do me good," rejoined Pierre de Moras, breathing more freely, "and yet I had already thought of all these things. But if she does not love now, she will some day—and suppose it should not be me! Were she to bestow upon another all that she refuses me! my friend," added the count, whose handsome features turned pale, "I would kill her with my own hand!"

"So much for being in love," said Lucan; "and I, am I nothing more to you, then?"

"You, my friend," said Moras with emotion, "you see my confidence in you! I have revealed to you weaknesses of which I am ashamed. Ah! why have I ever known any other feeling than that of friendship! Friendship alone returns as much as it receives; it fortifies instead of enervating; it is the only passion worthy of a man. Never forsake me, my friend; you will console me, whatever may happen."

The bell that was ringing for breakfast called them back to the chateau. Julia pretended being tired and ailing. Under shelter of this pretext, her silent humor, her more than dry answers to Lucan's polite questions, passed at first without awakening either her mother's or her husband's attention; but during the remainder of the day, and amid the various incidents of family life, Julia's aggressive tone and disagreeable manners toward Lucan became too strongly marked not to be noticed. However, as Lucan had the patience and good taste not to seem to notice them, each one kept his own impressions to himself. The dinner was, that day, more quiet than usual. The conversation fell, toward the end of the meal, upon extremely delicate ground, and it was Julia who brought it there, though, however, without the least thought of evil. She was exhausting her mocking *verve* upon a little boy of eight or ten—the son of the Marchioness de Boisfresnay—who had annoyed her extremely the night before, by parading through the ball his own pretentious little person, and by throwing himself pleasantly like a top between the legs of the gentlemen and through the dresses of the ladies. The marchioness went into ecstasies at these charming pranks. Clotilde defended her mildly, alleging that this child was her only son.

"That is no reason for bestowing upon society one scoundrel the more," said Lucan.

"However," rejoined Julia, who hastened to be no longer of her own opinion as soon as her step-father seemed to have rallied to it, "it is a well acknowledged fact that spoiled children are those who turn out the best."

"There are at least some exceptions," said Lucan, coldly.

"I know of none," said Julia.

"Mon Dieu!" said the Count de Moras in a tone of conciliation, "right or wrong, it is quite the fashion, nowadays, to spoil children."

"It is a criminal fashion," said Lucan. "Formerly their parents whipped them, and thus made men of them."

"When a man has such a disposition as that," said Julia, "he does not deserve to have any children—and he has none!" she added with a direct look that further aggravated the unkind and even cruel intention of her words.

Monsieur de Lucan turned very pale. Clotilde's eyes filled with tears. Julia, embarrassed at her triumph, left the room. Her mother, after remaining for a few moments, her face covered with her hands, rose from the table and went to join her.

"Now, *mon cher*," said Monsieur de Moras as soon as he found himself alone with Lucan, "what the mischief took place between you two last night? You did tell me something about it this morning, but I was so much absorbed in my own selfish preoccupations, that I paid no attention to it. But tell me, what did take place between you?"

"Nothing serious. Only I was able to satisfy myself that she had not yet forgiven my occupying a place which, according to her ideas, should never have been filled."

"What would you advise me to do, George?" rejoined Monsieur de Moras. "I am ready to do whatever you say.

"My dear friend," said Lucan, laying gently his hands upon Pierre's shoulders, "don't be offended, but life in common, under such conditions, becomes a very difficult matter. It is best not to wait until some irreparable scene. In Paris we will be able to see each other without difficulty. I advise you to take her away."

"Suppose she is not willing."

"I should speak firmly," said Lucan, looking him straight in the eyes; "I have some work to do this evening; it happens well and will give you a good opportunity. In the meantime, *au revoir.*"

Monsieur de Lucan locked himself up in his library. An hour later, Clotilde came to join him.

He could see that she had wept a great deal; but she held out her forehead to him with her sweetest smile. While he was kissing her, she murmured simply and in a whisper:

"Forgive her for my sake!"

And the charming creature withdrew in haste to hide her emotions.

The next morning, Monsieur de Lucan, who, as usual, had risen quite early, had been writing for some time near the library window, which opened at quite a moderate height on the garden. He was not a little surprised to see his step-daughter's face appear among the honeysuckle vines that crept over the iron trellis of the balcony:

"Monsieur," she said in her most melodious tone, "are you very busy?"

"Oh, not at all!" he replied, rising at the same time.

"It's because, you see, the weather is perfectly delightful," she said. "Will you come and take a walk with me?"

"Of course I will."

"Well, come then. Good Heavens! how sweet this honeysuckle does smell!"

And she snatched off a few flowers, which she threw to Lucan through the window, with a burst of laughter. He fastened them in his buttonhole, making the gesture of a man who understands nothing of what is going on, but who has no reason to be angry.

He found her in fresh morning costume, stamping upon the sand with her light and impatient foot.

"Monsieur de Lucan," she cries, gayly, "my mother wishes me to be amiable with you, my husband wishes it, Heaven wills it, too, I suppose; that's why I am willing also, and I assure you that I can be very amiable when I try. You'll see!"

"Is it possible?" said Lucan.

"You'll see, sir!" she replied, dropping him with all possible grace, a regular stage curtsey.

"And where are we going, pray, madam?"

"Wherever you like—through the woods, at random, if you please."

The wooded hills came so close to the chateau, that they bordered with a fringe of shade one side of the yard. Monsieur de Lucan and Julia took the first path that came in their way; but it was not long before Julia left the beaten roadway, to walk at hazard from tree to tree, wandering at random, beating the thickets with her cane, picking flowers or leaves, stopping in ecstasy before the luminous bands that striped here and there the mossy carpets, frankly intoxicated with movement, open air, sunshine, and youth. While walking, she cast to her companion words of pleasant fellowship, playful interpellation, childish jests, and caused the woods to ring again with the melody of her laughter.

In her admiration for the wild flowers, she had gradually collected a regular bundle, of which Monsieur de Lucan accepted the burden with cheerful resignation. Noticing that he was almost bending under the weight, she sat down upon the gnarled roots of an old oak, in order, she said, to make a selection among all this pell-mell. She then took upon her lap the bundles of grass and flowers, and began throwing out everything that appeared to her of inferior quality. She handed over to Lucan, seated a step or two from her, whatever she thought fit to retain for the final bouquet, justifying gravely her decision upon each plant that she examined:

"You, my dear, you are too thin! you're pretty, but too short! you, you smell bad! you, you look stupid."

Then, turning abruptly into another train of thought, which was not at first without causing some uneasiness to Monsieur de Lucan:

"It was you, wasn't it, who advised Pierre to speak to me with firmness?"

"I?" said Lucan, "what an idea!"

"It must have been you. You," she went on again, speaking to her flowers, "you look sickly, good-night! Yes, it must have been you. One might think you quite meek, to look at you, whereas, on the contrary, you are very harsh, very tyrannical."

"Ferocious!" said Lucan.

"At any rate, I have no fault to find with you for that. You were right; poor Pierre is too weak with me. I like a man to be a man. And yet he is very brave, is he not?"

"Extremely so," said Lucan; "he is capable of the most energetic actions."

"He looks like it, and yet with me—he is an angel."

"It is because he loves you."

"Quite probable!—some of those flowers are so curious. Look at this one; it looks like a little lady!"

"I hope that you love him too, my good Pierre?"

"Quite probable, too!"

After a pause, she shook her head:

"And why should I love him?"

"What a question!" said Lucan. "Why, because he is perfectly worthy of being loved; because he has every quality; intelligence, heart, and even beauty—finally, because you have married him."

"Monsieur de Lucan, will you allow me to tell you something confidentially?"

"I beg you to do so."

"That trip to Italy has been very injurious to me."

"In what way?"

"Before my marriage, I did not think myself positively ugly, but I fancied myself at least quite plain."

"Yes! Well?"

"Well! while traveling about Italy, among all those souvenirs and those marbles, so much admired, I made strange reflections. I said to myself that, after all, these princesses and goddesses of the ancient world, who drove shepherds and kings mad, for whose sake wars broke out and sacrileges were committed, were persons pretty much after my own style. Then occurred to me the fatal idea of my own beauty! I felt that I disposed of an exceptional power; that I was a sacred object that could not be given away for a vulgar trifle, and which could only be the reward—how can I say?—of a great deed or of a crime!"

Lucan remained for a moment astonished at the audacious

naivete of that language. He thought best, however, to laugh at it.

"But, my dear Julia," he said, "take care; you mistake the age. We are no longer in the days when nations went to war for the sake of a woman's pretty eyes. However, speak about it to Pierre; he has everything required to furnish the great action you want. As to the crime, I think you had better give it up."

"Do you think so?" said Julia. "What a pity!" she added, bursting out into a hearty laugh. "You see, I tell you all the nonsense that comes in my head. That's amiable enough, I hope, is it not?"

"It is certainly extremely amiable," said Lucan. "Keep on."

"With such precious encouragement, sir!" she said, rising and finishing her sentence with a courtesy; "but for the present, let us go to breakfast. I recommend my bouquet to your attention. Hold the head down. Walk ahead, sir, and by the shortest road, if you please, for I have an appetite that is bringing tears to my eyes."

Lucan took the path that led most directly to the chateau. She followed him with nimble step, at times humming a cavatina, at others addressing him fresh instructions as to the manner of holding her bouquet, or touching him lightly with the end of her cane, to make him admire some birds perched upon a branch.

Clotilde and Monsieur de Moras were waiting for them, seated upon a bench outside the gate of the chateau. The anxiety depicted upon their countenances vanished at the sound of Julia's laughing voice.

As soon as she saw them, she snatched the bouquet from Lucan's hands, ran toward Clotilde, and throwing on her lap her fragrant harvest:

"Mother," she said, "we have had a delightful walk—I had a great deal of fun; Monsieur de Lucan also, and what's more, he has improved very much by my conversation, I opened up new horizons to him!"

She described with her hand a great curve in the air, to indicate the immensity of the horizons she had opened up to Monsieur de Lucan. Then, drawing her mother toward the dining-room, and snuffing the air with apparent relish:

"Oh! that kitchen of my mother's!" she said. "What an aroma!"

This charming humor, which was a source of great rejoicing to all the guests of the chateau, never flagged during that entire day, and, most unexpected of all, it continued during the next and the following days without perceptible change. If Julia did still nurture any remnants of her moody cares, she had at least the kindness of keeping them to herself, and to suffer alone. More than once, still, she was seen returning from her solitary excursions with gloomy eye and clouded brow; but she shook off these equivocal dispositions as soon as she found herself again in the family circle, and was all amiability.

Toward Monsieur de Lucan particularly she showed herself most agreeable; feeling, probably, that she had many amends to make in that direction. She went so far as to take up a great deal of his time without much discretion, and to call him a little too often in requisition for walks or rides, for tapestry drawings, for playing duets with her, sometimes for nothing, simply to disturb him, standing in front of his windows, and asking him, in the midst of his reading, all sorts of burlesque questions. All this was charming; Monsieur de Lucan lent himself to it with the utmost good nature, and did not surely deserve great credit for doing so.

About this time, the Baroness de Pers came to spend three days with her daughter. She was at once advised, with full particulars, of the miraculous change that had taken place in Julia's character, and of her behavior toward her step-father. On witnessing the gracious attentions which she lavished upon Monsieur de Lucan, Madame de Pers manifested the liveliest satisfaction, in the midst of which, however, could be seen at times some slight traces of her former prejudices against her grand-daughter.

The day before the expected departure of the baroness, some of the neighbors were invited to dinner for her gratification, for she had but very little taste for the intimacy of family life, and was passionately fond of strangers. For want of time to do any better, they gave her for company, the cure of Vastville, the local physician, the receiver of taxes, and recorder of deeds, all of whom were tolerably frequent guests at the chateau, and great admirers of Julia. It was doubtless not a great deal; it was enough, however, to furnish to the baroness an occasion for wearing one of her handsome dinner-dresses.

Julia, during the dinner, seemed to make it a point to effect the conquest of the cure, a simple old man, who yielded to his fair neighbor's fascinations with a sort of joyous stupor. She made him eat, she made him drink, she made him laugh.

"What a little serpent she is, isn't she, Monsieur le Cure?" said the baroness.

"She is very lovely," said the cure.

"Enough to make one shudder," rejoined the baroness.

In the evening, after waltzing for a little while around the room, Julia, accompanied by her husband, sang in her beautiful, grave voice, some unpublished melodies and national songs she had brought back from Italy. One of these tunes having reminded her of a sort of tarentella she had seen danced by some women at Procida, she requested her husband to play it. She was explaining at the same time, with much animation, how this tarentella was danced, giving a rapid outline of the steps, the gestures and the attitudes; then, suddenly carried away by the ardor of her narrative:

"Wait a moment, Pierre," she said, "I am going to dance it. That will be much more simple."

She lifted the long train of her dress, which impeded her movements, and requested her mother to loop it up with pins. In the meantime she was right busy herself; there were on the mantelpiece, and on the consoles, vases filled with flowers and verdure; she drew freely from them with her nimble fingers, and, standing before a mirror, she fastened and twined pell-mell, in her magnificent hair, flowers, leaves, bunches, ears, anything that happened to fall under her hands. With her head loaded with that heavy and quivering wreath, she came to place herself in the center of the parlor.

"Go on now, dear!" she said to Monsieur de Moras. He played the tarentella, that began with a sort of slow and measured ballet-step, which Julia performed in her own masterly style, folding and unfolding in turn, like two garlands, her peri's arms; then the rhythm becoming more and more animated, she struck the floor with her rapid and repeated steps, with the wild suppleness and the wanton smile of a young bacchante. Suddenly she brought the performance to a close with a long slide that carried her, all panting, before Monsieur de Lucan, seated opposite to her. There, she bent one knee, lay with rapid gesture both her hands upon her hair, and tossing about at the same time her inclined head, she shook off her crown in a shower of flowers at the feet of Lucan, saying in her sweetest voice, and in a tone of gracious homage:

"There! sir!"

After which, she rose, and, still sliding, made her way to an arm-chair, into which she threw herself, and taking up the cure's three-cornered hat, she began to fan herself vigorously with it.

In the midst of the applause and the laughter that filled the parlor, the Baroness de Pers drew gently nearer to Lucan on the sofa which they were jointly occupying, and said to him in a whisper:

"Tell me, my dear sir, what in the world is the meaning of this new system? Do you know that I still preferred the old style myself?"

"How, dear madam? And why so?" said Lucan simply.

But before the baroness had time to explain, admitting that such was her intention, Julia was taken with another fancy.

"Really," she said, "I am smothering here. Monsieur de Lucan, do offer me your arm."

She went out, and Lucan followed her. She stopped in the vestibule to cover her head with her great white vail, seemed to hesitate between the door that led into the garden and that which led into the yard, and then deciding:

"To the Ladies' Walk," she said; "it's coolest there."

"The Ladies' Walk," which was Julia's favorite strolling resort, opened opposite the avenue, on the other side of the courtyard. It was a gently sloping path contrived between the rocky base of the wooded hill and the banks of a ravine that seemed to have been one of the moats of the old castle. A brook flowed at the bottom of this ravine with a melancholy murmur; it became merged, a little farther off, into a small lake shaded by willows, and guarded by two old marble nymphs, to which the Ladies' Walk was indebted for its name, consecrated by the local tradition. Halfway between the yard and the pond, fragments of wall and broken arches, the evident remnants of some outer fortification, rose against the hillside; for the space of a few paces, these ruins bordered the path with their heavy buttresses, and projected into it, together with festoons of ivy and briar, a mass of shade which night changed into densest darkness. It looked then as if the passage was broken by an abyss. The gloomy character of this site was not, however, without some mitigating features; the path was strewn with fine, dry sand; rustic benches stood against the bluff; finally, the grassy banks that sloped down into the ravine were dotted with hyacinths, violets, and dwarf roses whose perfume rose and lingered in that shaded alley like the odor of incense in a church.

It was then about the end of July, and the heat had been overpowering during the day. After leaving the atmosphere of the courtyard, still aglow with the fires of the setting sun, Julia breathed eagerly the cool air of the woods and of the brook.

"Dieu! how delightful this is!" she said.

"But I am afraid this may be a little too delightful," said Lucan; "allow me."

And he wound up in a double fold round her neck the floating ends of her vail.

"What! do you value my life, then?" she said.

"Most undoubtedly."

"That's magnanimous!"

She walked a few steps in silence, resting lightly upon the arm of her companion, and rocking, in her peculiar way, her graceful figure.

"Your good cure must take me for a species of demon," she added.

"He is not the only one," said Lucan, with ironical coldness.

She laughed a short and constrained laugh; then, after another pause, and while continuing to walk with downcast eyes:

"You must certainly hate me a little less now; say, don't you?"

"A little less."

"Be serious, will you? I know that I have made you suffer a great deal. Are you beginning to forgive me now?"

Her voice had assumed an accent of tenderness quite unusual to it, and which touched Monsieur de Lucan.

"I forgive you with all my heart, my child," he replied.

She stopped, and grasping his two hands:

"True? We will not hate each other any more?" she said, in a low and apparently timid tone. "You love me a little?"

"Thank you," said Lucan, with grave emotion; "thank you; I love you very much."

As she was drawing him gently toward her he clasped her in a frank and affectionate embrace, and pressed his lips upon the forehead she was holding up to him; but at the same instant he felt her supple figure stiffen; her head rolled back; then she sank bodily, and slipped in his arms like a flower whose stem has suddenly been mowed down.

There was a bench within two steps; he carried her there, but after laying her upon it, instead of affording her the required assistance, he remained in an attitude of strange immobility before that lovely and helpless form. A long silence followed, broken only by the gentle and monotonous ripple of the brook. Shaking off his stupor at last, Monsieur de Lucan called out several times in a loud and almost harsh voice:

"Julia! Julia!"

As she remained motionless still, he ran down into the ravine, took some water in the hollow of his hand, and bathed her temples with it. In the course of a minute or two, he saw her eyes opening in the darkness, and he helped her raise her head.

"What is it?" she said, looking at him with a wild expression; "what has happened, sir?"

"Why, you fainted," said Lucan, laughing.

"Fainted?" repeated Julia.

"Of course; that's just what I feared; you must have been benumbed by the cold. Can you walk? Come, try."

"Perfectly well," she said, rising and taking his arm.

Like all those who experience sudden prostration, Julia remembered, but in a very indistinct manner, the circumstance that had brought about her fainting.

In the meantime they had resumed their walk slowly in the direction of the chateau.

"Fainted!" she repeated, gayly; "mon Dieu! how perfectly ridiculous!"

Then, with sudden animation:

"But what did I say? Did I speak at all?"

"You said, 'I am cold!' and away you went!"

"Just like that?"

"Just like that."

"Did you think I was dead?"

"I did hope for a moment that you were," said Lucan, coldly.

"How horrid of you! But we were talking before that. What were we saying?"

"We were making a pact of amity and friendship."

"Well! it doesn't look much like it now, Monsieur de Lucan!"

"Madam?"

"You seem positively angry with me because I fainted."

"Of course I am. In the first place, I don't like that sort of adventures, and then, it is wholly your own fault; you are so imprudent, so unreasonable!"

"Oh! mon Dieu! Don't you want a switch?"

And as the lights of the chateau were coming into sight:

"*Apropos*, don't trouble mother with any of that nonsense, will you?"

"Certainly not; you may rest easy on that score."

"You are just as cross as you can be, you know?"

"Probably I am; but I have just spent there a few minutes so very painful."

"I pity you with all my heart," said Julia, dryly.

She threw off her vail in the vestibule, and returned to the parlor. The Baroness de Pers, who was to leave early the next day, had already retired. Julia performed some four-handed pieces on the piano with her mother. Monsieur de Lucan took the place of the "dummy" at the whist table, and the evening ended quietly.

CHAPTER VII.

Victory and Defeat.

The next morning, Clotilde was preparing to accompany her mother to the station in the carriage; Monsieur de Lucan, detained at the chateau by a business appointment, was present to take leave of his mother-in-law. He remarked the thoughtful countenance of the baroness; she was silent, much against her habit, and she cast embarrassed looks upon him; she approached him several times with a constrained smile and confidential manner, but confined herself to addressing to him a few commonplace words. Availing herself at last of a moment when Clotilde was giving some orders, she leaned out of the carriage-window, and, pressing significantly Monsieur de Lucan's hand:

"Be true and faithful to her, sir!" she said.

The carriage started almost immediately, but not before he had had time to notice that her eyes were filled with tears.

The matter that was engrossing Monsieur de Lucan's attention at the time, and on the subject of which he had had a long conversation that very morning with his lawyer and his advocate, who had come over from Caen during the night, was an old family lawsuit which the mayor of Vastville, an ambitious personage and restless busybody, had taken pride in bringing to light again. The question at issue was a claim for some public property the effect of which would have been to strip Monsieur de Lucan of a portion of his timbered lands and to curtail materially his patrimonial estate. He had gained his suit in the lower court, but an appeal was soon to be heard, and he was not without fears as to the final result. He had no difficulty in using that pretext, to account during the next few days, to the eyes of the inhabitants of the chateau, for a severity of physiognomy, a briefness of language, and a fondness for solitude, which concealed perhaps graver cares. That pretext, however, soon failed him. A telegram informed him, early the following week, that the suit had been finally decided in his favor, and he was compelled to manifest on this occasion an apparent joy that was far indeed from his heart.

He resumed from that moment the usual routine of family life to which Julia continued to impart the movement of her active imagination. However, he ceased to lend himself with the same affectionate familiarity to the caprices of his step-daughter. She noticed it; but she was not the only one who did. Lucan detected surprise in the eyes of Monsieur de Moras, reproaches in those of Clotilde. A new danger appeared before him; he was acting in a manner which it was equally impossible, equally perilous to explain or to allow being interpreted.

With time, however, the frightful light that had flashed across his brain in a recent circumstance was growing gradually fainter; it had ceased to fill his mind with the same convincing force. He conceived doubts; he accused himself at times on a veritable aberration; he charged the baroness with cruel and guilty prejudices; he thought, in a word, that, at all events, the wisest course was to avoid believing in the drama, and giving it life by taking a serious part in it. Unfortunately Julia's disposition, full of surprises and unforeseen whims, scarcely admitted of any regular plan of conduct toward her.

One beautiful afternoon, the guests of the chateau accompanied by a few of the neighbors, had gone on a horseback excursion to the extremity of Cape La Hague. On the return home, and when they had come about halfway, Julia, who had been remarkably quiet all day, left the principal group of riders, and, casting aside to Monsieur de Lucan an expressive glance, she urged her horse slightly forward. He overtook her almost immediately. She cast upon him again an oblique glance, and abruptly, with her bitterest and most incisive accent:

"Is my presence dangerous to you, sir?"

"How, dangerous?" he said, laughingly. "I do not understand you, my dear madam."

"Why do you avoid me? What have I done to you? What means this new and disagreeable manner which you affect toward me? It is really a very strange thing that you should become less polite to me, as I am more so to you. They persecute one for years to induce me to show you a pleasant countenance, and when I try my best to do so, you pout. What does it mean? What has got into your head? I should be infinitely curious to know."

"It is quite simple, and I am going to enlighten you in two words. It has got into my head that after being not very amiable to me, you are now almost too much so. I am sincerely touched and charmed at it; but I really fear, sometimes, to turn too much to my own profit attentions to which I am far from having the sole right. You know how fond I am of your husband. There can be no question of jealousy in this case, of course; but a man's love is proud and prompt to take umbrage. Without stooping to low and otherwise impossible sentiments, Pierre, seeing himself somewhat neglected, might feel offended and afflicted, at which we would both be greatly grieved, would we not?"

"I do not know how to do anything halfway," she said with a gesture of impatience. "How can I change my nature? It is with my own heart, and not with that of another, that I love and that I hate; and then, why should it not enter into my plans to excite Pierre's jealousy? My old traditional hatred for you has perhaps made this deep calculation; he would kill either you or me, and that would be as good a denouement as any other."

"You must allow me to prefer another," said Lucan, still trying, but without much success, to give a cheerful turn to this wildly passionate conversation.

"However," she went on, "you may rest easy, my dear sir. Pierre is not jealous. He suspects nothing, as they say in plays!"

She laughed one of her wicked laughs, and added at once in a graver tone:

"And what could he suspect? In being amiable toward you, I am merely acting under order, and no one can tell how much of it is genuine and how much put on."

"I feel quite certain that you don't know yourself," he said, laughingly. "You are a person of naturally restless disposition; you require agitation, and when there is none you try to imitate it as best as you can. Whether you like, or whether you don't like your stepfather, is not a very dramatic affair. There is no room here for any but very simple and very ordinary sentiments. It is well enough to complicate them a little—is it not, my dear?"

"Yes, my dear!" she said, emphasizing ironically the last word.

Whereupon she started her horse at a gallop.

They were then just reaching the edge of the woods. He soon saw her leave the direct road that led across them, and take a path over the heath as if intending to dash through the thickest of the timber. At the same instant Clotilde ran up to him, and touching his shoulder with the tip of her whip:

"Where in the world is Julia going?" she said.

Lucan replied with a vague gesture and a smile.

"I am sure," rejoined Clotilde, "that she is going to drink at that fountain, yonder. She was complaining a little while since of being thirsty. Do follow her, dear, will you, and prevent her doing so. She is so warm! It might be fatal to her. Run, I beg of you."

Monsieur de Lucan gave the reins to his horse, and he started like the wind. Julia had already disappeared under cover of the woods. He followed her track; but among the timber, the roots and the roughness of the ground somewhat checked his speed. At a short distance, in the center of a narrow clearing, the labor of ages and the filtrations of the soil had hollowed out one of those mysterious fountains whose limpid water, moss-grown banks, and aspect of deep solitude delight the imagination, and give rise to so many poetic legends. When Monsieur de Lucan was able once more to see Julia, she had alighted from her horse. The admirably trained animal stood quietly two or three steps away, browsing the young foliage, while his mistress, down on her knees and stooping over the edge of the spring, was drinking from her hands.

"Julia, I beg of you!" exclaimed Monsieur de Lucan in an imploring tone.

She started to her feet with a sort of elastic spring, and greeted him gayly.

"Too late, sir!" she said; "but I only drank a few drops, just a few little wee drops, I assure you!"

"You must really be out of your mind!" said Lucan who was by this time quite close to her.

"Do you think so?"

She was shaking her beautiful white hands, which had served her for a drinking-cup, and which seemed to throw off a shower of diamonds.

"Give me your handkerchief!"

Lucan handed her his handkerchief. She wiped her hands gravely; then, as she returned the handkerchief with her right hand, she raised herself on tiptoe and held her left hand up to the level of his face:

"There! now; don't scold any more!"

Lucan kissed the hand.

"The other now," she said again. "Please don't turn so pale, sir!"

Monsieur Lucan affected not to have heard these last words, and came down abruptly from his horse.

"I must help you to mount," he said, in a dry and harsh voice.

She was putting on her gloves with downcast look. Suddenly raising her head and looking at him with fixed gaze:

"What a miserable wretch I am, am I not?" she said.

"No," said Lucan; "but what an unhappy being!"

She leaned against one of the trees that shaded the spring, her head partially thrown back and one hand over her eyes.

"Come!" said Lucan.

She obeyed, and he assisted her to get on her horse. They rode out of the wood without uttering another word, made their way to the road, and soon overtook the cavalcade.

As soon as he had recovered from the anguish of that scene, Monsieur de Lucan did not hesitate to think that the departure of Julia and of her husband must be the immediate and inevitable consequence of it; but when he came to seek some means of bringing about their sudden departure, his mind became lost in difficulties that he could not solve. What motive could he indeed offer to justify, in the eyes of Clotilde and of Monsieur de Moras, a determination so novel and so unexpected? It was now the middle of August, and it had been agreed for a long time that the entire family should return to Paris on the first of September. The very proximity of the time fixed upon for the general departure would only serve to make the pretext invoked to explain this sudden separation appear more unlikely. It was almost impossible that it should not awaken in the mind of Clotilde, and in that of the count, irreparable suspicions and a light fatal to the happiness of both. The remedy seemed indeed more to be dreaded than the evil itself; for, if the evil was great, it was at least unknown to those whose lives and whose hearts it would have shattered, and it could still be hoped that it might remain so forever. Monsieur de Lucan thought for a moment of going away himself; but it was still more impossible to justify his departure than it was that of Julia's.

All these reflections being made, he resolved to arm himself with patience and courage. Once in Paris, separate dwellings, less frequent intercourse, the obligations of the world, and the activity of life, would doubtless afford relief and then a peaceful solution to a painful and formidable situation which it was henceforth impossible for him not to view in its true light. He relied upon himself, and also upon Julia's natural generosity, for reaching without outburst and without rupture the approaching term that was to put an end to their life in common and to its incessant perils. It ought not to be impossible to endure, for the short period of two weeks more, the threatenings of a storm that had been brewing for months without revealing its lightning. He was forgetting with what frightful rapidity the maladies of the soul, as well as those of the body, after reaching slowly and gradually certain stages, suddenly precipitate their progress and their ravages.

Monsieur de Lucan asked himself whether he should not inform Julia of the conduct he had resolved to follow, and of the reasons that had dictated it; but every shadow of an explanation between them appeared to him eminently improper and dangerous. Their confidential understanding upon such a subject would have assumed an air of complicity which was repugnant to all his sentiments of honor. Despite the terrible light that had flashed forth, there still remained between them something obscure, undecided, and unconfessed that he thought best to preserve at any cost. Far, therefore, from seeking opportunities for some private interview, he avoided them all from that moment with scrupulous care. Julia seemed penetrated with the same feeling of reserve, and anxious to the same degree as himself to avoid any *tête-à-tête*, while striving to save appearances; but in that respect she did not dispose of that power of dissimulation which Lucan owed to his natural and acquired firmness. He was able, without visible effort, to hide under his habitual air of gravity the anxieties that consumed him. Julia did not succeed, without an almost convulsive restraint, in carrying with bold and smiling countenance the burden of her thought. To the only witness who knew the secret of her struggles, it was a poignant spectacle to behold the gracious and feverish animation of which the unhappy child sustained the appearance with so much difficulty. He saw her sometimes at a distance, like an exhausted comedienne, retiring to some isolated bench in the garden, and fairly panting with her hand pressing upon her bosom, as if to keep down her rebellious heart. He felt then, in spite of all, overcome with immense pity in presence of so much beauty and so much misery.

Was it only pity?

The attitude, the words, the looks of Clotilde and of Julia's husband were at the same time, for Monsieur de Lucan, the objects of constant and uneasy observation. Clotilde had evidently not conceived the slightest alarm. The gentle serenity of her features remained unaltered. A few oddities, more or less, in Julia's ways did not constitute a sufficient novelty to attract her particular attention. Her mind, moreover, was too far away from the monstrous abysses yawning at her side; she might have stepped into them and been swallowed up, before she had suspected their existence.

The blonde, placid, and handsome countenance of the Count de Moras retained at all times, like Lucan's dark face, a sort of sculptural firmness. It was, therefore, rather difficult to read upon it the impressions of a soul which was naturally strong and self-controlling. On one point, however, that soul had become weak. Monsieur de Lucan was not ignorant of the fact; he was aware of the count's ardent love for Julia, and of the sickly susceptibility of his passion.

It seemed unlikely that such a sentiment, if it were seriously set at defiance, should not betray itself in some violent or at least perceptible exterior sign. Monsieur de Lucan, in reality, was unable to observe any of these dreaded symptoms. If he did occasionally surprise a fugitive wrinkle on his brow, a doubtful intonation, a fugitive or absent glance, he might believe at most in some return of that vague and chimerical jealousy with which he knew the count to have been long tormented. Besides, he saw him carrying into their family circle the same impassive and smiling face, and he continued to receive from him the same tokens of cordiality. Oppressed, nevertheless by his legitimate scruples of loyalty and friendship, he had for one moment the mad temptation of revealing to the count the trial that was imposed upon them; but while revealing his own heart, would not such a delicate and cruel confession break the heart of his friend? And, moreover, would not such a pretended act of loyalty, involving the betrayal of a woman's secret, be tainted with cowardice and treason?

It was necessary, therefore, amid so many dangers and so much anxiety, to sustain alone, and to the end, the weight of that trial, more complicated and more perilous still, perhaps, than Monsieur de Lucan was willing to admit to himself.

It was to come to an end much sooner than he could possibly have anticipated.

Clotilde and her husband, accompanied by Monsieur and Madame de Moras, went one day, in the carriage, to visit the ruins of a covered gallery which is one of the rarest of druidical antiquities in the country. These ruins lay at the back of a picturesque little bay, scooped out in the rocky wall that borders the eastern shore of the peninsula. Their shapeless masses are strewn over one of those grass-clad spurs that extend here and there to the foot of the cliff like giant buttresses. They are reached, despite the steepness of the hill, by an easy winding road that leads, with long, meandering turns, down to the yellow, sandy beach of the little bay. Clotilde and Julia made a sketch of the old Celtic temple while the gentlemen were smoking; then they amused themselves for some time watching the rising waves spreading upon the sand its fringes of foam. It was agreed to return to the top of the hill on foot in order to relieve the horses.

The carriage, on a sign from Lucan, started ahead. Clotilde took the arm of Monsieur de Moras, and they began ascending slowly the sinuous road. Lucan was waiting Julia's good pleasure before following them; she had remained a few steps aside, engaged in animated conversation with an old fisherman who was busy setting his bait in the hollow of the rocks. She turned toward Lucan, and slightly raising her voice:

"He says there is another path, much shorter and quite easy, close by here, along the face of the cliff. I am strongly inclined to take it and avoid that tiresome road."

"Believe me, do nothing of the kind," said Lucan; "what is a very easy path for the country people may prove a very arduous one for you and even for me."

After further conference with the fisherman:

"He says," rejoined Julia, "that there is really no danger, and that children go up and down that way every day. He is going to guide me to the foot of the path, and then I'll only have to go straight up. Tell mother I'll be up there as soon as you all are."

"Your mother will be dreadfully anxious."

"Tell her there is no danger."

Lucan, giving up the attempt to resist any longer a fancy that was growing impatient, went up to the footman who carried Julia's album and shawl; he requested him to reassure Clotilde and Monsieur de Moras, who had already disappeared behind one of the angles of the road; then returned to Julia.

"Whenever you are ready," he said.

"You are coming with me?"

"As a matter of course."

The old fisherman preceded them, following close to the foot of the cliffs. After leaving the sandy beach of the bay, the shore was covered with angular rocks and gigantic fragments of granite that made walking extremely painful. Although the distance was very short, they were already breaking down with fatigue when they reached the entrance to the path, which appeared to Lucan, and perhaps to Julia herself, much less safe and commodious than the fisherman had pretended. Neither one nor the other, however, attempted to make any objection. After a few last recommendations and directions, their old guide withdrew, quite pleased with Lucan's generosity. Both began then resolutely to scale the cliff which, at this point of the coast, is known as the cliff of Jobourg, and rises some three hundred feet above the level of the ocean.

At the beginning of this ascension, they broke the silence they had hitherto maintained, in order to exchange some jesting remarks upon the charms and comforts of this goat's-path; but the real and even alarming difficulties of the road soon proved sufficient to absorb their entire attention. The faintly beaten path disappeared at times on the barren rock, or under some recent landslide. They had much trouble finding the broken thread again. Their feet hesitated upon the polished surface of the stone, or the short and slippery grass. There were moments when they felt as if they stood upon an almost vertical slope, and if they attempted to stop and take breath, the vast spaces stretching before them, the boundless extent, the dazzling and metallic brilliancy of the sea, caused them a sensation of dizziness and as of a floating motion. Though the sky was low and cloudy, a heavy and storm-laden heat weighed upon them and stimulated the action of their blood. Lucan walked first, with a sort of feverish excitement, turning around from time to time to cast a glance at Julia, who followed him closely, then looking up to see some resting-point, some platform upon which they might breathe for a moment in safety. But above him, as below, there was naught save the perpendicular and sometimes overhanging cliff. Suddenly Julia called out to him in a tone of anguish:

"Monsieur! monsieur! please, oh! please—my head is whirling!"

He walked rapidly back a few steps at the risk of tumbling down, and, grasping her hand energetically:

"Come! come!" he said, with a smile, "what is the matter?—a brave person like you!"

"It would require wings!" she said, faintly.

Lucan began at once to climb the path again, supporting and almost dragging Julia, who had nearly fainted.

He had at last the gratification of setting his foot upon a projection of the ground, a sort of narrow esplanade jutting from the rock. He succeeded in drawing Julia upon it. But she sank at once in his arms, and her head rested upon his chest. He could hear her arteries and her heart throbbing with frightful force. Then, gradually, her agitation subsided. She lifted her head gently, opened her long eyelashes, and looking at him with rapturous eyes:

"I am so happy!" she murmured; "I wish I could die so!"

Lucan pushed her off from him the length of his arm, then, suddenly seizing her again and clasping her tightly to his heart, he cast upon her a troubled glance, and then another upon the abyss. She certainly thought they were about to die. A slight tremor passed across her lips; she smiled; her head half rolled back:

"With you?" she said—"what happiness!"

At the same moment, the sound of voices was heard a short distance above them. Lucan recognized Clotilde's and the count's voices. His arm suddenly relaxed and dropped from Julia's waist. He pointed out to her, without speaking, but with an imperious gesture, the path that wound around the rock.

"Without you, then!" she said, in a gentle and proud tone. And she began ascending.

Two minutes later, they reached the plateau above the cliff, and related to Clotilde the perils of their ascension, which explained sufficiently their evident agitation. At least they thought so.

During the evening of this same day, Julia, Monsieur de Moras, and Clotilde were walking after dinner under the evergreens of the garden. Monsieur de Lucan, after keeping them company for a short time, had just retired, under pretense of writing some letters. He remained, however, but a few minutes in the library, where the sound of the others' voices reached his ears and disturbed his attention. A desire for absolute solitude, for meditation, perhaps also some whimsical and unaccountable feeling, led him to that very ladies' walk stamped for him with such an indelible recollection.

He walked slowly through it for some time, in the deepening shades with which the falling night was rapidly filling it. He wished to consult his soul, as it were, face to face, to probe like a man his mind to its utmost depths. What he discovered there terrified him. It was a mad intoxication, which the savor of crime further heightened. Duty, loyalty, honor, all that rose before his passion to oppose it only exasperated its fury. The pagan Venus was gnawing at his heart, and instilling her most subtle poisons into it. The image of the fatal beauty was there without truce, present in his burning brain, before his dazzled eyes; he inhaled with avidity and in spite of himself, its languor, its perfume, its breath.

The sound of light footsteps upon the sand caused him to suspend his march. He caught through the darkness a glimpse of a white form approaching him.

It was she!

Without giving scarce a thought to the act, he threw himself behind the obscure angle formed by one of those massive pillars that supported the ruins against the side of the hill. A mass of verdure made the darkness there more dense still. She went by, her eyes fixed upon the ground, with her supple and rhythmical step. She walked as far as the little pond that received the waters of the brook, stood dreaming for a few moments upon its edge, and then returned. A second tune she went by the ruins, without raising her eyes, and as if deeply absorbed. Lucan remained convinced that she had not suspected his presence, when suddenly she turned her head slightly around, without interrupting her march, and she cast behind her that single word, "Farewell," in a tone so gentle, so musical, so sorrowful, that it was somewhat like the sound of a tear falling upon a sonorous crystal.

That minute was a supreme one. It was one of those moments during which a man's life is decided for eternal good or for eternal evil. Monsieur de Lucan felt it so. Had he yielded to the attraction of passion, of intoxication, of pity, that was urging him with almost irresistible force on the footsteps of that beautiful and unhappy woman—that was on the point of casting him at her feet, upon her heart—he felt that he became at once and forever a lost and desperate soul. Such a crime, were it even to remain wholly ignored, separated him forever from all he had ever respected, all he had ever held sacred and inviolate; there was nothing left for him either upon earth or in heaven; there was no longer any faith, probity, honor, friend, or God! The whole moral world vanished for him in that single instant.

He accepted her farewell, and made no reply. The white form moved away and soon disappeared in the darkness.

The evening was spent in the home circle as usual. Julia, pale, moody, and haughty, worked silently at her tapestry. Lucan observed that on taking leave of her mother she was kissing her with unusual effusion.

He soon retired also. Assailed by the most formidable apprehensions, he did not undress. Toward morning only, he threw himself all dressed upon the bed. It was about five o'clock, and scarcely daylight as yet, when he fancied he heard muffled steps on the carpet, in the hall and on the stairs. He rose again at once. The windows of his room opened upon the court. He saw Julia cross it, dressed in riding costume. She went into the stable and came out again after a few moments. A groom brought her her horse, and assisted her in mounting. The man, accustomed to Julia's somewhat eccentric manners, saw apparently nothing alarming in that fancy for an early ride. Monsieur de Lucan, after a few minutes of excited thought, took his resolution. He directed his steps toward the room of the Count de Moras. To his extreme surprise, he found him up and dressed. The count, seeing Lucan coming in, seemed struck with astonishment. He fastened upon him a penetrating and visibly agitated look.

"What is the matter?" he said, at last, in a low and tremulous voice.

"Nothing serious, I hope," replied Lucan. "Nevertheless, I am uneasy. Julia has just gone out on horseback. You have, doubtless, seen and heard her as I have myself, since you are up."

"Yes," said Moras, who had continued to gaze upon Lucan with an expression of indescribable stupor; "yes," he repeated, recovering himself, not without difficulty, "and I am glad, really very glad to see you, my dear friend."

While uttering these simple words, the voice of Moras became hesitating; a damp cloud obscured his eyes.

"Where can she be going at this hour?" he resumed with his usual firmness of speech.

"I do not know; merely some new fancy, I suppose. At any rate, she has seemed to me lately more strange, more moody, and I feel uneasy. Let us try and follow her, if you like."

"Let us go, my friend," said the count after a pause of singular hesitation.

They both left the chateau together, taking their fowling-pieces with them, in order to induce the belief that they were going, according to a quite frequent habit, to shoot sea-birds. At the moment of selecting a direction, Monsieur de Moras turned to Lucan with an inquiring glance.

"I see no danger," said Lucan, "save in the direction of the cliffs. A few words that escaped her yesterday lead me to fear that the peril may be there; but with her horse, she is compelled to make a long detour. By cutting across the woods, we'll be there ahead of her."

They entered the timber to the west of the chateau, and walked in silence and with rapid steps.

The path they had taken led them directly to the plateau overlooking the cliffs they had visited the previous day. The woods extended in that direction in an irregular triangle, the last trees of which almost touched the very brink of the cliff.

As they were approaching with feverish steps that extreme point, Lucan suddenly stopped.

"Listen!" he said.

The sound of a horse's gallop upon the hard soil could be distinctly heard. They ran.

A sloping bank of moderate elevation divided the wood from the plateau. This they climbed half way with the help of trailing branches; screened then by the bushes and the foliage, they beheld before them a most impressive spectacle. At a short distance to the left, Julia was coming on at breakneck speed; she was following the oblique line of the woods, apparently shaping her course straight toward the edge of the cliff. They thought at first that her horse had run away, but they saw that she was lashing him with her whip to further accelerate his speed.

She was still some hundred paces from the two men, and she was about passing before them. Lucan was preparing to leap to the other side of the bank, when the hand of Monsieur de Moras fell violently upon his arm and held him back—firmly.

They looked at each other. Lucan was amazed at the profound alteration that had suddenly contracted the count's features and sunken his eyes; he read at the same time in his fixed gaze an immense sorrow, but also an immovable resolve. He understood that there was no longer any secret between them. He yielded to that glance, which, so far as he was concerned—he felt sure of that—conveyed nothing but an expression of confidence and friendly supplication. He grasped his friend's hand within his own and remained motionless. The horse shot by within a few steps of them, his flanks white with foam, while Julia, beautiful, graceful, and charming still in that terrible moment, sat lightly upon the saddle.

Within a few feet of the edge of the cliff, the horse, scenting the danger, shied violently and wheeled around in a semicircle. She led him back upon the plateau, and, urging him both with whip and voice, she started him again toward the yawning chasm.

Lucan felt Monsieur de Moras' nails cutting into his flesh. At last the horse was conquered; the ground gave way under his hind feet, which only met the vacant space. He fell backward; his fore legs pawed the air convulsively.

The next moment the plateau was empty. No sound had been heard. In that deep chasm the fall had been noiseless and death instantaneous.

THE END

www.ingramcontent.com/pod-product-compliance
Lightning Source LLC
Chambersburg PA
CBHW030517260626
47157CB00005B/1780